SANÂTANA DHARMA

An Advanced Textbook of Hindu Religion and Ethics

SANAGE
PUBLISHING HOUSE

Paperback: 978-939089612-7

Printed by: Manipal Technologies Limited, Manipal

Sanage Publishing House LLP
Mumbai, India

sanagepublishing@gmail.com

Central Hindu School, formerly known as **Central Hindu College**, is one of India's largest schools which is situated at Kamachha in the heart of the holy city Varanasi.

सत्यमेव जयते नानृतम् ॥

उत्तिष्ठत जाग्रत प्राप्य वरान्निबोधत ॥

CONTENTS

PART I
BASIC HINDU RELIGIOUS IDEAS

PART II
GENERAL HINDU RELIGIOUS CUSTOMS AND RITES

PART III
ETHICAL TEACHINGS

FOREWORD

The Board of Trustees of the Central Hindu College has laid down the following principles on which religious and moral teaching is to be given in all institutions under its control.

The object of the Central Hindu College being to combine Hindu religious and ethical training with the western education suited to the needs of the time, it is necessary that this religious and ethical training shall be of a wide, liberal and unsectarian character, while at the same time it shall be definitely and distinctively Hindu. It must be inclusive enough to unite the most divergent forms of Hindu thought, but exclusive enough to leave outside it, forms of thought which a wide, lndu. It must avoid all doctrines which are the subject of controversy between schools recognised as orthodox; it must not enter 'nto any of the social and political questions of the day; but it must lav a solid foundation of religion and ethics on which the student may build, in his manhood, the more specialised principles suited to his intellectual and emotional temperament. It must be directed to the building up of a character—pious, dutiful, strong, self-reliant, upright, righteous, gentle and well-balanced—a character which will be that of a good man and a good citizen; the fundamental principles of religion, governing the general view of life and of life's obligations, are alone sufficient to form such a character. That which unites Hindus in a common faith must be clearly and simply taught , all that divides them must he ignored. Lastly, care must be taken to cultivate a wide spirit of tolerance, which not only respects the differences of thought and practice among Hindus, but which also respects the differences of religion among non Hindus, regarding all faiths with reverence, as roads whereby men approach the Supreme.

Therefore:—

1. The reiigious and ethical instruction must be such as all Hindus can accept.
2. It must include the special teachings which mark out Hinduism from other religions.
3. It must not include the distinctive views of any special school or sect.

This elementary Text-Book, written in accordance with this scheme, is intended for the use of Hindu boys in the middle and upper sections of the High Schools of India, and is designed to give them a general but correct idea of their national religion, such as may be filled in by fuller study in College and in later life, but will not need to be changed in any essential respect

It contains the fundamental ideas and doctrines which are generally received as orthodox, but does not enter into the details as to which sectarian divisions have arisen. It is believed that while a sectarian parent or teacher will probably make additions to it, he will not find in it anything which he will wish positively to repudiate.

While the book may be placed in the hands of the hoys for their own study, it is intended to be simplified by the oral explanations of the teacher, and each chapter serves as an outline on which one or more lessons may be based.

The shlokas given at the end of the chapters should be committed to memory by the boys. They will thus acquire a useful store of sacred authorities on their religion.

The name of this series, *Sanatana Dharma,* was chosen after full discussion, as best representing the idea of the fundamental truths presented. It has become somewhat of a sectarian name in some parts of India, but it is here taken only as meaning the eternal religion.

That this book may prove useful in laying a firm foundation of right thinking in the minds of Hindu youths, and may help in shaping them into pi ms, moral, loyal and useful citizens of their Motherland and of the Empire, is the prayer with which its compilers send it forth to the world.

PART I

BASIC HINDU RELIGIOUS IDEAS

ॐ

मंगलं दिशतु नो विनायको
मंगलं दिशतु नः सरस्वती।
मंगलं दिशतु नः समुद्रजा
मंगलं दिशतु नो महेश्वरी ॥

INTRODUCTION

Sanatana Dharma means the Eternal Religion, the Ancient Law, and it is based on the Vedas, sacred books given to men many long ages ago. This Religion has also been called the Aryan Religion, because it is the Religion that was given to the first nation of the Aryan race; Arya means noble, and the name was given to a great race, much finer in character and appearance than the races which went before it in the world's history. The first families of these people settled in the northern part of the land now called India, and that part in which they first settled was named Aryavarta, because these Aryans lived in it. "(The land) from the eastern ocean to the western ocean, between the two mountains (Himavan and Vindhya) the wise call Aryavarta."

In later days the Religion was called the Hindu Religion, and this is the name by which it is now usually known. It is the oldest of living Religions, and no other Religion has produced so many great men—great teachers, great writers, great sages, great saints, great kings, great warriors, great statesmen, great benefactors, great patriots. The more you know of it, the more you will honour and love it, and the more thankful you will be that you were born into it. But unless you grow up worthy of it, this great and holy Religion will do you no good.

THE BASIS OF SANATANA DHARMA

The Ancient Religion is based on one strong foundation on which are erected the walls of its structure.

The foundation is called श्रुतिः Shrutih "that which has been heard the walls are called स्मृतिः Smrtih, "that which has been remembered."

The s has been given through very wise men, who heard it and received it from Devas; these sacred teachings were not written down till comparatively modern times, but were learnt by heart, and constantly repeated.

The teacher sang them to his pupils, and the pupils sang them after him, a few words at a time, over and over again, till they knew them thoroughly. Boys still learn the Shruti in the same way as their forefathers learnt it in very ancient days, and you may hear them chanting it in any Vaidika Pathashala at the present time,

The Shruti consists of the चतुर्वेदाः Chaturvedah, the Four Vedas. Veda means knowledge, that which is known; and the knowledge which is the foundation of Religion is given to man in the Four Vedas. They are named: ऋग्वेदः *Rigvedah;* सामवेदः *Samavedah*;;जुर्वेदः V*ajurvedah;* and अर्थर्ववेदः *Atharvavedah.*

Each Veda is divided into three parts:

1. मन्त्रः Mantrah; or संहिता Samhita, collection
2. ब्राह्मणाम् Brahmanam.
3. उपनिषत् Upanishat.

The Mantra portion consists of Mantras, or sentences in which the order of sounds has a particular power, produces certain effects. These are in the form of hymns to the Devas—whose relations to men we shall study presently—and when they are properly chanted by properly instructed persons, certain results follow. These are used in religious ceremonies, and the value of the ceremony depends chiefly upon their proper repetition.

The Brahmana portion of the Vedas consists of directions about ritual and explains how to perform the ceremonies in which were used the Mantras given in the first part; and further, stories connected with them.

The Upanishat portion consists of deep philosophical teachings on the nature of Brahman, on the supreme and the separated Self, on man and the universe, on bondage and liberation. It is the foundation of all philosophy, and when you are men, you may study it and delight in it. Only highly educated men can study it; it is too difficult for others.

There was a fourth part of the Veda in the ancient days, sometimes called the उपवेदः Upavedah, or तन्त्रम् Tantram; this consisted of science, and of practical instructions based on the science; but very little of the true ancient Tantra remains, as the Rishis took them away as unsuitable for times in which people were less spiritual. Some Tantrika forms of ritual are, however, used in worship, along with, or instead of, the current Vaidika forms. The books now extant under the name of Tantras are generally not regarded as part of the Veda.

That which is found in the Shruti is of supreme authority and is accepted by every faithful follower of the Sanatana Dharma as final. All the sects, all the philosophical systems, appeal to the Shruti as the find authority, determining every dispute.

The Smriti or Dharma Shastra, is founded on, and stan is next in authority to, the Shruti, and consists of four great works, written by Sages, the chief contents of which are laws and regulations for the carrying on of individual, family, social and national life. Hindu Society is founded on, and governed by, these laws. They are: —

1. **मनुस्मृतिः** or **मानवधर्मशास्त्रं** *Manu Smrtih* or *Manava Dharma Shastram. The Institutes of Manu.*

2. **याज्ञवल्क्यस्मृतिः** *Yajnavalkya Smrtih.*
3. **शंखलिग्वितस्मृतिः** *Shankha Likhita Smrtih.*
4. **पगशरस्मृतिः** *Parasha.ra Smrtih.*

The first of these is the chief compendium of Aryan law, Manu being the great Law-giver of the race. Hindu chronology divides the history of a world into seven great periods or cycles of time, each of which is begun and is ended by a Manu, and is therefore called a Manvantara, Manu-antara, "between (two) Manus."

"Six other Manus, very great-minded and of great splendour, belonging to the race of this Manu, the descendant of Svayambhu, have each produced beings." As there are two Minus for each Manvantara, that shows that we are in the fourth Manvantara, under the rule of the seventh Manu, who is, the next shloka tells us, the son of Vivasvat. Some of his laws are handed down in the *Manu Smrtih.*

The *Yajnavalkya Smrtih* follows the same general line as the *Manu Smrtih* and is next in im portance to it. The other two are not now much studied or referred to, except in some parts of Southern India.

While the Shruti and the Smriti are the foundation and the walls of the Sanatana Dharma, there are two other important supports like buttresses; the **पुराणानि,** Puranani, Puranas, and the **इतिहासः** Itihasah, History.

The Puranas consist of histories and stories and allegories, composed for the use of the less learned part of the nation, especially for those who could not study the Vedas. They are very interesting to read, and are full of information of all kinds. Some of the allegories are difficult to understand, and require the help of a teacher.

The Itihasa comprises two great poems:

1. The **रामायणम्** *Romayanam,* the history of Shri Ramachandra, the son of King Dasharatha, and of His wife Sita, and

of His brothers, a most interesting and delightful story, as you all know.

2. The महाभारतं, *Mahabharatam,* the history of the Kurus, a royal family of Northern India, which split into two parties, the Kurus and the Pandavas, between whom a great war broke out. It contains an immense number of beautiful stories, noble moral teachings, and useful lessons of all kinds.

These two books, the *Ramavana* and the *Mahabhrata*, tell us most of what we know about ancient India, about her people and customs, and her ways of living, and her arts, and her manufactures. If you read these, you will learn how great India once was, and you will also learn how you must behave to make her great once more.[1]

THE SCIENCE AND PHILOSOPHY OF SANATANA DHARMA

While the Shruti and the Smriti, the Puranas and the Itihasa make the edifice of Hindu Religion, we find that the Religion itself has given rise to a splendid literature of Science and Philosophy.

The Science was divided into the षडंगानि Shadangani, the Six Angas, literally Limbs; and these six Limbs, or Branches, comprised what would now be called secular knowledge. In the old days religious and secular knowledge were not divided.

They included Grammar, Philology, Astrology, Poetry, together with sixty-four sciences and arts, and the method by which study should be carried on, so that any one who mastered the six angas was a man of varied and deep learning.

The Philosophy also had six divisions, the षड्दर्शनानि Shaddarshanani, the Six Darshanas, or ways of seeing things,

---

1 Summaries of these have been given as lectures at the C. H. College, by Annie Besant, and are published as *The Story of the Great War, and Shri Ramachandra.*

usually called the Six Systems. They all have one object: the putting an end to pain by enabling the separated human selves to re-unite with the supreme Self; and they all have one method—the development of ज्ञानम् *Jnunam,* Wisdom. The ways employed are different, to suit the. different mental constitutions of men, so that they are like six different roads, all leading to one town.

As to what is contained in the Six Systems of philosophy, it will be enough for boys to know this:

The Nyaya and the Vaisheshika arrange all the things of the world into a certain number of kinds; then point out that a man knows all things by means of his senses, or by inference and analogy, or by testimony of other (wise and experienced) men; and then they explain how God has made all this material world oat of atoms and molecules; finally they show how the highest and most useful knowledge is the knowledge of God, who is also the inmost Spirit of man, and how this knowledge is obtained in various ways.

The Sankhya explains in more detail and in new ways the nature of पुरुषः Purushah, Spirit, and of प्रकृतिः Prakritih. Matter, and relation of each to the other.

The Yoga says that as there are now generally known five senses and five organs of action, so there are other subtler senses and organs; and explains more fully how they may be developed by men who are seeking to know God, who is their own true inmost Spirit.

The Mimansa explains what karma is, *i. e.,* action, both religious and worldly, and what are its consequences, causes and effects, and how it binds man to this world or to another.

The Vedanta finally tells fully what is the exact and true nature of God, or Atma. and shows that Jiva of man is in essence the same as this inmost God, and explains how man may live so that karma shall not bind him; and finally, by understanding what the Maya Shakti of God is, by which all this world comes forth and appears and disappears, how he may (after practice of Yoga) merge himself into and become one with God and so gain Moksha

CHAPTER 1

THE ONE EXISTENCE

There is one Infinite Eternal, Changeless Existence, the All.

From That all comes forth; to That all returns.

"One only, without a second."[2]

That includes within Itself all that ever has been, is, and can be. As a wave rises in the ocean, a universe rises in the All. As the wave sinks again into the ocean, a universe sinks again into the All. As the ocean is water, and the wave a form or manifestation of the water, so is there one Existence, and the universe is a form, or manifestation, of the Existence. "All this verily (is) Brahman."[3]

This is the primary truth of Religion. Men have given to the All many different names The name in the Sanatana Dharma is Brahman. English-speaking people use the name God, adding, to make the meaning clear, God, in His own Nature." Sometimes the Hindu speaks of the All as Nirguna Brahman, the Brahman without attributes, or the unconditioned Brahman. This is to distinguish the unmanifested state of Brahman, the All, from the manifested state, in which Brahman is called the Saguna Brahman, the Brahman with attributes, or the conditioned Brahman the Supreme Ishvara with His universe.

These, are called: "the two state® of Brahman;" the subject is very difficult, and it is enough for a boy to understand that

2 *Chhandogyop,* VI, ii—I.

3 *Ibid,* III, xiv—i, "This" is the technical name for a universe.

the Saguna Brahman is Brahman revealed—not "a second," but Brahman shining forth as The One, the Great Lord of Being, Thought and Bliss. He is the self-existent One, the Root and Cause of all beings. He is also sometimes called Purusottama. the Supreme Spirit, The Self. With Himself as Spirit He reveals the other side of the All, which is named Mulaprakriti, the Root of Matter. Prakriti, Matter, is that which takes form, and so can give bodies of all sorts and shapes and kinds; all that we can touch, taste, smell, see, and hear, is Matter, and a great deal more besides, which our live senses are not yet developed enough to perceive. The solids, liquids and gases of the chemist are made of Matter; all the things round us, stones, trees, animals, men, are made of Matter. But the whole of them is not Matter; inaudible, invisible, unsmellable, untastable, intangible, the Spirit is in each, an अंशः Amshah, a portion, of Ishvara. We call the Matter part a शरीरम् Shariram, body; or a कोषः koshah,[4] sheath; or an उपाधिः Upadhih, vehicle; that which embodies, clothes, or carries the Spirit. Thus Ishvara is in everything, and it is He who gives life to all things. He is आत्मा Atma, the Self, the Immortal, the Inner Ruler, dwelling in all objects, and there is nothing that can exist apart from Him. An amshah of Him in a body of matter is called a Jiva, or a Jivatma, a separated Self.

There are some very important differences between Spirit and Matter, as well as the differences just spoken of: that the senses, when completely developed, can perceive Matter, while they cannot perceive Spirit, and that Matter takes form while Spirit is formless. It is the Spirit that is life, and that thinks, and feels, and observes, that is the "I" in each of us. And the Spirit is one and the same in everybody and in everything But Matter cannot think, or feel, or observe; it is जडं Jadam, without consciousness. And it has also the tendency to be constantly dividing itself into many forms and to become many. So that Spirit and Matter are said to be the

4 Spelt also कोषः koshah.

opposites one of the other; Spirit is called the knower, the one that knows, while Matter is called the object of knowledge, that which is known.

Students should try to understand these differences, and must never confuse Spirit and Matter; they are opposites, the first "pair of opposites," out of which a universe is built up.

Just as Spirit has three qualities, सत् चित् आनन्दं—Sat Chit Anandam—Being, Thought-Power and Bliss, so has Matter three qualities तमः रजः सत्वम् Tamah, Rajah, Sattvam-Inertia, Mobility, Rhythm. Inertia gives resistance and stability to Matter; Mobility keeps Matter active, moving about; Rhythm makes the movements regular. You may say: "A stone does not move of itself." But science tells you that every particle in that stone— particles too small for you to see—is moving rapidly and regularly to and fro, is vibrating, to use the scientific term.

The शक्तिः Shaktih, or the Divine Power of Ishvara, which makes Matter begin to take form, is called माया Maya, and sometimes दैवीप्रकृतिः Daiviprakrtih, the Divine Prakrti. Shri Krshna speaks of "My Divine Prakrti " as "My other Prakrti, the higher, the life-element, by which the universe is upheld."[5]

The student may think of the great pair of opposites, Ishvara and Mulaprakrti, standing, as it were, face to face and the Divine Power of Ishvara shining out on Mulaprakrti and making the qualities, called गुणाः gunah, act on each other, so that many forms begin to appear. This Divine power is Maya, and so Ishvara is called the Lord of Maya.

Even young students must try to remember these names, and what they mean, for they cannot otherwise understand the teaching of the *Bhagavad Gita*, which every Hindu boy must try to understand. It may be well to say that the word Prakrti is generally used instead of Mulaprakrti, the prefix Mula. Root, being usually left out.

---

5 Bhagavad Gita, vii—5.

क्षेयंयप्तत् प्रवक्ष्यामियज्ञात्वाऽमृतमश्नुते ।
श्रनाांदमत् परं ब्रह्म न सत् नन्नासदुच्यत ॥
सर्वतः पाणिपादं नत् सर्वतांऽक्षिशिगेमुखम् ।
सर्वतः श्रुतिमल्लोके सर्वमावृत्य तिष्ठनि ॥
सर्वोंद्रियगुणाभासं सर्वेन्द्रियाविवर्जितम् ।
असक्तं सर्वभृच्चैव निर्गुणप्र गुएाभोक्त च ॥
बहिरन्तश्च भूतानामचरं चरमेव च ।
सूक्ष्मत्वात् तदविक्षेयं दूरस्थ्र चान्तिके च तत् ॥
त्मविमकं च भूतेषू विभकमिव च स्थितम् ।
भूतभर्तृ च तज्शेयं ग्रसिष्णु प्रभविष्णु च ॥
ज्योतिषामपि तज्ज्योतिस्तमसः परमुच्यतं ।
ज्ञानं श्रेयं ज्ञानगम्यं हृदि सर्वस्य विष्ठितम् ॥[6]

"I will declare that which ought to be known, that which being known immortality is enjoyed— the beginningless supreme Brahman, culled neither Being nor Not-Being.

"Everywhere That has hands and feet, every-where eyes, heads and mouths; all hearing, He dwelleth in the world, enveloping all;

"Shining with all sense-faculties, without any sense; unattached, supporting everything; and free from qualities, enjoying qualities.

"Without and within all beings, immovable and also movable; by a reason of his subtlety indistinguishable; at hand and far away is That.

"Not divided amid beings and yet seated distributatively. That is to be known as the supporter of beings; He devours and He generates.

That, the Light of all lights, is said to be beyond darkness; wisdom, the object of wisdom, by wisdom to be reached, seated in the hearts of all."

6 *Bhagavad Gita*, xiii,12—17.

श्रासीदिदं नमोभूतम प्रज्ञातमलच्चणाम् ।
श्रप्रतर्क्य मविक्षेयं प्रसुप्तामिव सर्वतः ॥
ततः स्वयंभूर्मगवानव्यक्तो व्यज्जयन्नदम् ।
महाभूतादि वृत्तौजाः प्रादुरासीत्तमोनुदः ॥
योऽसावतोन्द्रियग्राह्मः सूदमांऽव्यक्तः सनातनः ।
सर्वभूत मयोऽरिचन्त्यः स एवं स्वंयमुद्‌बभौ ॥[7]

This was in the form of Darkness, unknown, without marks [or homogeneous], unattainable by reasoning, unknowable, wholly, as it were, in sleep.

"Then the self-Existent, the Lord, unmanifest, (but) making manifest. This—the great elements and the rest—appeared with mighty power, Dispeller of Darkness.

"He who can be grasped by that which is beyond the senses, subtle unmamifest, ancient, containing all beings, inconceivable, even He Himself shone forth."

अहमात्मा गुड़ांकश सर्वभूताशय स्थितः ।
श्रहमादिश्च मध्यं च भूतानामन्त एव च ॥[8]

"I, O Gudakesha, am the Self, seated in the heart of all beings; I am the beginning, the middle, and also the end of all beings."

द्वाविमौ पुरुषो लोके त्तृगश्चक्षर एव च ।
त्तृरः सर्वारी भूतानि कूटस्थोऽत्तृर उच्यते ॥
उत्तमः पुरुषस्त्वन्यः विभर्त्त्यव्यय ईश्वरः ॥
यस्मात् त्तृरमतीतोऽहमत्तृरढ़पि चोत्तमः ।
श्रतोऽस्मि लोके वेदे च प्रथितः पुरुषोत्तमः ॥[9]

7 *Manu smriti i—5, 6, 7.*

8 Bh*agavad Gita, x*—2O.

9 *Ibid*, xv—1O.

"There are two Purushas in this world, the destructible and the indestructible; the destructible is all beings, the unchanging is called the Indestrueτible.

"The highest Purusha is verily another, declared as the Supreme Self; He who pervading all, sustaineth the three worlds, the indestructible Ishvara.

"Since I excel the destructible, and am more excellent also than the indestructible, in the world and in the. Veda I am proclaimed Prushottama."

ममेवांशो जीवलोके जीवभूतः सनातनः ।
मनः षष्ठानीन्द्रियाणि प्रकृतिस्थानि कर्षाति ॥[10]

"A portion of Mine own Self, transformed in the world of life into an immortal Spirit, draweth round itself the senses, of which the mind is the sixth, veiled in matter."

समं सर्वेषु भूतंषु तिष्ठन्तं परमेश्वरम् ।
विनश्यत्स्वत्रिनश्यन्तंयः पश्यति स पश्यति ॥
यदा भूत पृथग्भावमें क स्थमनू पश्यति ।
तत एव च विम्तांर ब्रह्म सम्पद्यते तदा ॥
यथा प्रकाशयत्येकः कृत्स्नं लोकमिमं रविः ।
क्षेत्रं क्षेत्री तथा कृत्स्नं प्रकाशयति भारत ॥[11]

"Seated equally in all beings, the supreme Ishvara, unperishing within the perishing; he who thus seeth, he seeth.

"When he preceiveth the diversified exsitence of beings as rooted in One and spreading forth from It, then he reacheth Brahman.

---

10 Bhagavad Gita, xv—7.

11 *Ibid* xiii—27 30, 33.

"As the one sun illumineth the whole earth so the Lord of the field, illumineth the whole field, O Bharata."

भूमिरापोऽनलो वायुः खं मनो बुद्धिरेव च ।
अहंकार इतीयं में मित्रा प्रकृतिरष्टधा ॥
श्रपरंयमितस्त्वन्यां प्रकृति विद्धि मे पराम् ।
जीवभूतां महावाहोययेदं धार्यते जगत् ॥[12]

"Earth, Water, Eire, Air, Other, Mind and Reason also and Egoism—these are the eight-fold divisions of my Prakrti.

"This the inferior. Know my other Prakrti, the higher, the life-element, O mighty-armed, by which the universe is upheld."

सत्वं रजस्तम इति गुणाः प्रकृति सम्भवाः ।
निबध्नन्ति महाबाहो देहे देहिनमव्ययम् ॥[13]

"Sattva, Rajas, Tamas, these are the Gunas, born of Prakriti; they bind fast in the body, O great-armed one, the indestructible dweller in the body."

CHAPTER 2

THE MANY

When Ishvara shines out on Prakriti and makes it fall into shapes, the first Forms that appear are those of the त्रिमूर्त्तिः Trimurtih, the three Aspects of Ishvara, manifested to cause a ब्रह्मराडं Brahmandam, *literally* an Egg of Brahma, a universe, or orderly system of worlds. The aspect of Ishvara in which He creates the

12 B*hagavad-Gita,* vii 4-5.

13 *Ibid*—xiv—5

worlds is named Brahma; Brahma is the Creator. The aspect of Ishvara in which He preserves, takes care of, and maintains the worlds is named Vishnu; Vishnu is the Preserver. The aspect of Ishvara in which He dissolves the worlds, when they are worn out and of no further use, is named Shiva, or Mahadeva; Shiva is the Dissolver of the worlds. These are the first manifestations of Ishvara, His Supreme Forms, His three Aspects, or Faces. The One, the Saguna Brahman, or the Supreme Ishvara, appears as Three.

Brahma, the Creator, shapes matter into seven तत्त्वानि Tattvani, Elements, as they have been called.r[14] Different names are given to the first two; we may use the names Mahat-Buddhi, Pure Reason, and Abamkara, Egoism, the principle of separation, breaking up matter into tiny particles, colled atoms. Then come the remaining five Tattvas: Akasha, Ether; Vayu, Air; Agni, Fire; Apa, Water; Prithivi, Earth. This is called the creation of the Bhutadi, Elements, and out of these all things are partly made. There is more of Tamo-guna than of Rajo-guna and of Sattva-guna showing itself in these elements, and so the things composed chiefly of them are dull and inert; the inner life, the Jiva, cannot show its powers, for the coat of matter is so thick and heavy.

Next after the Elements, the ten Indriyas are created; these were at first only ideas in the mind of Brahima, and later were clothed in the Elements; they are the five centres of the senses: smell, taste, sight, touch, hearing, the organs of which are the nose, tongue, eyes, skin and ears; and the five centres of action, the organs of which are hands, feet, and those of speech, generation and excretion. There is more of Rajo-guna than of Tamo-guna and of Sattva-guna shewing itself in these Indriyas, so they are very active, and the. inner life, the Jiva, can show more of its powers in them.

---

14 The western chemist Uses the word in a different sense, but the old meaning is the one we are concerned with.

After the Indriyas, Brahma created in His mind the Devas who are connected with the senses, and also Manah, the mind, which is sometimes called the sixth Indriya, when the first five are spoken of, and the eleventh, when the ten are taken; because it draws into itself and arranges and thinks over all the sensations collected by the Indriyas from the outer world. There is more of Sattva-guna than of Tamo-guna and of Rajo-guna showing itself in these Deities and Manah.

The student must remember that these gunas are never separated, but one guna may be more dominant than another in any particular being. When Tamo-guna dominates, the being is called tamasik; when Rajo-guna dominates, the being is called rajasik; when Sattva-guna dominates, the being is called sattvik. All things may be divided under these three heads of sattvik, rajasik, and tamasik.[15]

Brahma next created in His mind the hosts of Devas, who carry out, administer the laws of Ishvara, and see to the proper management of all the worlds. Ishvara is the King, the One Lord, and the Devas are His ministers, like the ministers and officials of an earthly king. The students must never confuse the Devas With the supreme Ishvara. with Brahman. They are His higher officials for the Brahmanda, as we men are His lower officials for this one particular world.

The Devas, sometimes called Suras, see that each man gets what he has earned by his karma.[16] They give success and failure in worldly things, according to what a man deserves; they help men in many ways, when men try to serve them, and much of the bad weather and sickness and famine and other national troubles come from men entirely neglecting the duties they owe to the Devas. The Devas are a vast multitude, divided under their five Rulers, Indra, Vayu, Agni, Varuna and Kubera. Indra has to do

---

15 *See Bhagavad-Gita*, xiv, xiv and xviii.

16 Karma is explained in Chapter IV.

with the ether; Vayu with the air; Agni with the fire; Varuna with the water; Kubera Avith the. earth. The Devas under each have different names, as we see in the Puranas and the Itihasa. The student may have read, for instance, how Bhima fought with the Yakshas, who were the servants of Kubera.

In these Devas the Rajo-guna dominate; Manu says that their "nature is action."

The Asuras, the enemies of the Devas, embody the resistance, or inertia, of Matter, and in them Tamo-guna is predominant.

Brahma then created in His mind minerals, plants, animals and men, thus completing the picture o£ the worlds wherein the unfolding of the powers of the Jiva—what is now called Evolution —was to take place. In Sanskrit this world-evolution, or world-process, is called संसार Samsarah, and it is compared to a wheel, constantly turning, on which all Jivas are bound.

Thus Brahma completed His share of the great task of a universe, but the forms needed, to he clothed in physical matter, to be made active beings; this was the work of Vishnu, the All-pervader, the Maintainor and Preserver of the worlds. He breathed His Life into all these forms, and, as a Purana says, became Prana in all forms and gave them consciousness. Then all the Brahmanda "became full of life and consciousness." But even this was not enough, when man came upon the scene. Two Aspects of Ishvara had given Their Life, but the third Aspect remained, the One who dissolves forms and thus liberates the Jivas, calling them to union and bliss. The life of Mahadeva must be poured out to complete the triple Jiva of man, that he might be the perfect reflexion of the triple Ishvara. This was done, and the human Jiva began his long evolution, having already passed through, evolved through, the mineral, vegetable and animal kingdoms in previous kalpas. A very beautiful description of the evolution through plants and animals to men, until "in man Atma is manifest," and "by the mortal he desires the immortal," may be read by elder students in the *Aitareyaranyaka,*[17] and will be found in the *Advanced Text-Book.*

The special manifestations of Vishnu, called Avataras, must not be forgotten. The word means One who descends, from *tri* passing over, the prefix "ava" giving the significance of descending. It is applied to Divine manifestations of a peculiar kind, in which the Deity incarnates in some form to bring about some special result. When things are going badly with the world, and special help is needed to keep the world on the road of right evolution, then Vishnu comes down in some appropriate form, and puts things right.

Ten of His Avataras are regarded as more important than the others, and are often spoken of as "the Ten Avataras."

1. Matsya, the fish.—Vaivasva.a Manu once saw a little fish, gasping for water, and put it into a bowl; it grew, and He placed it in a larger pot; then again in a larger, and then in a tank, a pond, a river, the sea, and ever the Fish grew and filled its receptacle. Then the Manu knew that this Fish was connected with His own life-work, and when the time came for Him to save the seeds of life from a great flood, He entered a ship with the Rishis and the necessary life-seeds, the great Fish appeared, and drew the vessel to the world where lay the Manu's work. With the coming of the Fish began the great evolution of animal life in the world.
2. Kurma, the Tortoise.—As the tortoise, Vishnu, supported the whirling mountain, which churned the great sea of matter, that it might give forth the necessary forms. The Tortoise is the type of the next great step in evolution.
3. Varaha, the Boar.—The earth was sunk below the waters, and Vishnu raised it up, giving, in the Boar, the type of the great mammalian kingdom which was to flourish on the dry land.

17 II, iii—2.

Modern Science recognises these three great stages of evolution, each marked in Hinduism by an Avatara.

4. Narasimua, the Man-Lion.—This was the Avatara that came to free the earth from the tyranny of the Daityas. Into this race a child, Prahlada, was born, who from earliest childhood was devoted to Vishnu, despite the threats and the cruelties of his Diatya father. Over and over again the father tried to slay the son, but ever Vishnu intervened to save him; at last He burst from a pillar in the form of a Man-Lion, and slew the Daitya King.
5. Vamana, the Dwarf.—At last He came as mar, to aid the evolution of the human race, and gained from Bali the right to all He could cover, in three steps; one step covered the earth, and thus He won for man the field of his evolution.
6. Parashurama, Rama of the Axe.—This Avatara came to punish such of the Kshttriyas as were oppressing the people, and to teach bad rulers the danger of using power to tyrannise, instead of to help.
7. Rama, usually called Ramachandra, the son of Dasharatha.—He, with His three brothers, came as the ideal Kshattriya, the model King, and He serves as an example of a perfect human life. An obedient and loving son, a tender husband, an affectionate brother, a gallant warrior, a wise ruler, a diligent protector of His people, He is emphatically The Perfect Man. His splendid story Is told in Valmiki's *Ramaynnam,* and the lovely version of Tulsi Das is known in every northern Indian home.
8. Krishna, the manifestation of Divine Love and Wisdom, worshipped by myriads with intense devotion.—As the marvellous child of Vraja and Vrindavana, as the friend of Arjuna, as the speaker of the *Bhagavad-Gita*, as the wise counsellor of the Pandavas, as the adored of Bhishma—

what Indian boy does not know His story? He is the central Figure of the *Mahabhartam* and His Life is traced in several Puranas.

9. Buddha, the gentle prince who gave up throne and luxury to become a travelling mendicant, Teacher of the Truth.— He is known as Shakyamuni, as Gautama, as Siddhartha, and is the founder of a mighty faith, followed by millions of the human race. In him Vishnu teaches vast multitudes of non-Aryan peoples.

10. Kalki—the Avatara who shall close the Kali Yuga, and whose coming is yet in the future. When He comes, the Satya Yuga, will return to earth, a new cycle will begin.

The development and perfection of the human type is indicated by these Avataras.

पश्यामि देवांस्तव देव देहे
सर्वांस्तथा भूतविशेषसंघान् ।
ब्रह्मरामीशं कमलासनस्थं
ऋषींश्व सवांनुरगांश्च दिव्यान् ॥
रुद्रादित्या बसवोये च साध्या
विश्वेऽविश्वनौ मरुतश्चोष्मपाश्च।
गन्धर्वयत्तृासुरसिद्धसंघा
वीक्षन्ते त्वां विस्मिताश्चैव सर्वे ॥[18]

"Within Thy Form, O God, the Gods I see,
All grades of being with distinctive marks;
Brahma the Lord, upon His lotus-throne,
The Rishis all, and Serpents, the Divine.
Rudras, Vasus, Sadhyas and Adityas,
Vishvas, the Ashvins, Maruts, Ushmapas,

18 *Bhagavad-Gita,* xi, 15 and 22.

Gandharvas, Yakshas, Siddhas, Asuras,
In wondering multitudes beholding Thee."

इन्द्रं मित्रं वरुणामग्निमाहु-
रथो दिव्यः स सुपर्णो गरुत्मान् ।
एक सद्विप्रा बहुधा वद्न्ति
श्रग्निंयमं मातरिश्वानमाहुः ॥[19]

"Indra, Mitra, Varuna, Agni, they call him, and He is the radiant golden-feathered Garutman, Of Him who is one, Sages speak as manifold; they call him Agni, Yama, Matarishva."

आत्मैव देवताः सर्वाः सर्वमात्मन्यवस्थितम् ।[20]

"All the Gods (are) even the Self: all rests on the Self.

एतमेके वदन्त्यग्निमनुमन्ये प्रजापतिम् ।
इन्द्रमेकेऽपरे प्रारामपरे ब्रह्म शाश्वतम् ॥[21]

"Some call Him Agni, others Manu, (others) Prajapati, some Indra, others Life-Breath, others the eternal Brahman."

यथा सुदीप्तात्पावकाद्विस्फुलिङ्गाः
सहस्त्रशः प्रभवन्ते सरूपाः ।
तथात्तृराद्विविधाः सौम्य भावाः
प्रजायन्ते तत्र चैवापियान्ति ॥
....
एतस्माज्जयते प्राणो मनः सर्वेन्द्रियणि च ।

19 Rigreda, I. clxiv. 46
20 *Manusmriti*, xii 119
21 *Ibid*, 124.

स्त्रं वायुर्ज्योतिरापः पृथिवी विश्वस्य धारिणी ॥

....

तस्माच्च देवा बहुधा सम्प्रसूताः
साध्या मनुष्या पशवो पयाँसि ।[22]

"As from a blazing fire sparks, all similar to each other, spring forth in thousands so from the Indestructible, O beloved, various types of being are born, and they also return thither.........

"From That are born Breath, Mind, and all the Senses, Ether, Air, Fire, Water, and Earth, the support of all..........

"From that in various ways are born, the Gods, Sadhyas, Men, Beast, Birds.

सत्त्वात् संजायते ब्रानं रजसो लोभ एव च ।
प्रमादमोहौ तमसो भवतोऽज्ञानमेव च ॥
ऊर्ध्वं गच्छन्ति सत्त्वस्था मध्ये तिष्ठन्ति राजसाः ।
जघन्यगुणावृत्तिस्था श्रधो गच्छन्ति तामसाः ॥[23]

"From Sattva wisdom is born, and also greed from Rajah; negligence and delusion are of Tamah, and also unwisdom.

"They rise upwards who are settled in Sattva; the Rajasic dwell in the midmost place. The Tamasic go downwards, enveloped in the vilest qualities."

सत्त्वं सुखे ससुयति रजः कर्माणि भारत ।
ज्ञानमावृत्य तु तमः प्रमादे सञ्जयत्युत ॥
रजस्तमश्चाभिभूय सत्त्वं भवति भारत ।
रजः सत्त्वं तमश्चैव तमः सत्त्वं रजस्तथा ॥

---

22 *Mundakop, 11, i, 1—17.*

23 *Bhagavad-Gita*, xiv, *17. 18.*

सर्वद्वारेषु देहेऽस्मिन् प्रकाश उपजायते ।
ज्ञानंयदा तदा विद्याद् विवृद्धे सत्वामित्युत ॥
लोभः प्रवृत्तिरारम्भः कर्मगाऽमशमः स्पृहा ।
रजस्येतानि जायन्ते जायन्ते विवृद्धे भरतर्षभ ॥
श्रप्रकाशोऽप्रवृत्तिश्च प्रमादो मोह एव च ।
तमस्येतानि जायन्ते विवृद्धे कुरुनन्दन ॥[24]

"Sattva attacheth to bliss, Rajah to action, O

Bharata. Jamah, verily, having shrouded wisdom, attacheth on the contrary, to heedlessness.

(Now) Sattva prevaileth, having overpowered Rajah and Tamah, O Bharata; (now) Rajah (having overpowered) Tamas and Sattva, (now) Jamas, (having overpowered) Rajah and Sattva.

"When the wisdom-light streameth forth from all the gates of the body, then it may be known that Sattva is increasing.

"Greed, outgoing energy, undertaking of actions, restlessness, desire—these are born of the increase of Rajah, O best of the Bharatas.

"Darkness, stagnation and heedlessness, and also delusion—these are born of the increase of. Tamah, O joy of the Kurus."

यदायदा हि धर्मस्य ग्लानिर्भवति भारत ॥
अभ्युत्थानमघर्मस्य तदात्मानं सृजाम्यहम् ॥
परित्राणाय साधूनां विनाशाय च दुष्कृताम् ॥
धर्मसंस्थापनार्थाय सम्भ्वामियुगेयुगे ॥[25]

"When dharma decays, when adharma is exalted then I Myself come forth;

24 *Bhagavad-Gita*, xiv, 9—13.

25 *Bhagavad-Gita,* iv, 7.—5.

For the protection of the good, for the destruction of evil-doers, for firmly establishing dharma, I am born from age to age."

CHAPTER 3

RE-BIRTH

The evolution spoken of in the last chapter is carried on by the Jiva passing from body to body, the bodies improving as his powers unfold; this is called re-birth, re-incarnation, or transmigration. The word re-incarnation means literally taking flesh again, coming again into a physical body. The word transmigration means passing from one place to another—passing into a new body. Either word can be used equally well. Let us see what is the process described by these words.

The Jiva, we have seen, is a portion of Brahman, "a portion of myself, a Jiva,'' says Shri Krshna. He contains the powers of Brahman, is Brahman. "Thou art That," the Shruti teaches. But yet there is a difference in Space and Time, as the seed is different from the tree. The tree produces a seed, giving it its own nature; it drops the seed on the ground, and the seed slowly grows, putting out its hidden powers, until it becomes a tree like its parent; it *can become nothing else,* because its nature is the same as that of the parent. And so with the Jiva; like a seed he is dropped into matter by Ishvara, he slowly grows, putting out his hidden powers, until he becomes Ishvara; he *can become nothing else*, because his nature is the same as that of his Parent, Ishvara.

Ishvara is said to be wise and powerful, Jiva to be unwise and powerless;[26] but the Jiva grows into wisdom and power, and that growth is what is called Evolution.

We have seen that the Jiva begins in the mineral kingdom his long pilgrimage through the physical world. At that stage

26 Shvetashvatarop, i—9.

he is unconscious of the outer world. His attention is called to it, its existence is forced on him, by violent shocks and blows from outside; earthquakes, volcanoes, landslips, the rolling or the furious surf, these and many other violent agencies arouse the Jiva's attention to the fact that he is not alone, that there is something outside him. If the student reads the accounts of the very early periods of the earth's history, he will be struck by the number of big catastrophies; all these were necessary to awaken the Jivas. After a very very long time, the Jivas were sufficiently awake to be fit for softer and more flexible bodies than minerals, and they went on into plants, while others, coming out later from Ishvara, took their places in the mineral kingdom.

The Jivas in the plants now became more conscious of the outer world, feeling the warm sun, and the gentle breezes, and the life-giving rain. As they grew older and more sensitive, they passed into the longer-lived plants, such as shrubs and trees, and in these more of their inner powers unfolded, till they were ready to go on into the animal kingdom, while the younger ones came on into the vegetable kingdom, and others still younger into the minerals.

And now in the animal kingdom the Jivas got on much faster, and by hunting for food, and fighting and outwitting each other, the senses and the simple mental powers were brought out and strengthened; until at last the animal forms were no longer good enough for them, and they needed the human in order that their evolution should not stop.

The student may ask: What makes the forms evolve to suit the Jiva? The Jiva's own efforts. He wants to look out through the wall of matter that encloses him; he tries to see, and his outwardgoing energy works on the wall, and slowly, very very slowly, evolves an eye; and so with all the senses and all the organs. The senses are pierced from within outwards, we are taught. The Jiva shapes them all to suit himself, so that he can use his powers in the outer world, and the Devas help him by giving him materials that are suited to the organ he wants to build. When he is trying to see, Agni gives him some of his own fiery matter, which vibrates when touched by rays of light. When he wants to taste, Varuna gives him some of his own watery matter, which makes tasting possible. And so on. In this way he makes his bodies, and when he has shaped one as much as he can, and it is of no further use to him, he throws it away and makes another. He evolves faster and faster as he goes on, because his powers, as they work more freely, can bring about results much more quickly than in the earlier stages.

This is the general process of evolution, and the succession has been told about as though it were unbroken, so that the student may grasp the main idea. But, in nature, while the general stream is onwards, there are many little twists and turnings and runnings up into bye-ways. A Jiva may slip backwards for a time, stay a while in a stage that he has long left behind him. There is something he has not quite learned, some power he has not quite evolved, and he falls by this into a lower stage again as a boy at school, if he were idle, might be put back into a lower class. A Jiva which has reached the human stage may be attached to an animal, or to a plant, or, if he be *very* tamasic, even to a stone, till he has learned to use the human form better. Then he is like a man in prison, shut out from human society, and unable to use his human powers, for want of freedom.

But the Jiva is not to be tied for ever to the wheel of births and deaths. The ropes that tie him to this wheel are his desires. So long as he desires objects that belong to this earth, he must come back to this earth in order to possess and enjoy these objects. But when he ceases to desire these objects, then the. ropes are broken, and he is free. He need not be born any more; he has reached liberation. He is then called a Mukta, a free Jiva.

Often Muktas remain in this world to help its progress, so that other Jivas may get free sooner than they otherwise would. We read about such Muktas in the Vedas and Puranas and the Itihasa; sometimes they are great Rishis or Kings, and sometimes they are quite simple people. But whatever they may be. in outside appearance, they are pure and unselfish and calm, and live only to help others. They are content to labour for the good of the world, and they know that they are one with Ishvara.

देहिनोऽस्मिन्यथा देहे कौमारंयौवनं जरा ।
तथा देहान्तरप्राप्तिधर्रिस्तत्र न मुह्यति ॥[27]

"As the dweller in the body experienceth, in the body, childhood, youth and old age, so passeth he on to another body. The steadfast one grieveth not thereat."

श्रन्तवन्त इमे देहा नित्यस्योक्ताः शरीरिणाः ।
श्रनाशिनोऽप्रमेयस्य तस्मादूयुध्यस्व भारत ॥
य एनं वेति ह्न्तारंयश्चैनं मन्यते हतम् ।
उभौ तौ न विजानीतो नायं हन्ति न हन्यते ॥
न जायतं म्रियरा वा कदाचन्-
नायं भूत्वा भविता वा न भूयः ।
श्रजो नित्यः शाक्ष्वतोऽयं पुराणो
न हन्यते हन्यमाने शरीरे ॥
वेद!विनाशिनं नित्यंय एनमजमध्ययम् ।
कथं स पुरुषः पार्थ ! कंघातयति हन्ति कम् ! ॥
वासांसि जीर्णानियथा विहाय
नवानि गृह्नाति नरोऽपराणि ।
तथा शरीराणि विहाय जीर्णा-
न्यन्यानि संयाति नवानि देही ॥

27 *Bhagavad- Gita,* ii—*13*

देही नित्यमवध्योऽयं देहे सर्वस्य भारत ।
तस्मात् सर्वाणि भूतानि न त्वं शेचितुमर्हसि ।।[28]

"These bodies of the embodied One who is eternal, indestructible and boundless, are known as finite. Therefore light, O Bharata.

"He who regardeth this as a slayer, and he who thinketh he is slain, both of them are ignorant. He slayeth not, nor is he slain.

"He is not born, nor doth he die: nor, having been, ceaseth he any more to be; unborn, perpetual. eternal and ancient, he is not slain when the body is slaughtered.

"Who knoweth him indestructible, perpetual, unborn, undiminishing, how can that man slay, O Partha, or cause to be slain?

"As a man, casting off worn-out garments, taketh new ones, so the dweller in the body, easting off worn-out bodies, entereth into others that are new.

"This dweller in the body of every one is ever invulnerable, O Bharata. Therefore thou shouldst not grieve for any creature."

तद्यथा पेशस्कारी पेशसो मात्रामुपादायान्यन्नवतरं कल्या-
णतरं स्त्रां तनुत एवमेवायमात्मेदं शरीरं निहत्याविद्यां
गमयित्वान्यन्नवतरं कल्याणातंर कल्याणातरंरूपं कुरुते ।।[29]

"As a goldsmith, having taken a piece of gold, maketh another form, new and more beautiful, so verily the Atma, having cast off this body and having put away Avidya, maketh another new and more beautiful form."

ब्रह्मरायाधाय कर्माणि संगं त्यक्त्वा करोतियः ।
लिप्यते न से पापेन पद्मपत्रमिवाम्भसा ।।

28 *Bhagavad-Gita*, ii, *18-22 and 30.*

29 *Brihadaranyakop*, IV, iv—4,

कायेन मनसा वुद्धया केवलैरिन्द्रियैरपि ।
योगिनः कर्म कुर्वन्ति संगं त्यक्त्वाऽऽत्मशुद्धये ॥
युक्तः कर्मफलं त्यक्त्वा शान्तिमाप्नोति नैष्टिकीम् ।
अयुक्तः कामकरेणा फले सक्तो निबध्यते ॥[30]

"He who acteth placing all actions in Brahman, abandoning attachment, is unaffected by sin, as a lotus leaf by the waters.

"Yogis, having abandoned attachment, perform action only by the body, by the mind, by the reason, and even by the senses, for the purification of the self.

"The harmonised man, having abandoned the fruit of action, attaineth to the eternal peace; the non-harmonised, impelled by desire, attached to fruit, are bound."

विद्याविनयसम्पन्न ब्राह्मणो गवि हस्तिनि ।
शुनि चैव श्रवपाके च पणिडताः समदर्शिनः ॥
इहैव तैर्जितः सर्गोयेष्य्र साम्ये स्थितं मनः ।
निर्दोषं हि समं ब्रह्म तस्माद् ब्रह्मणि ते स्थिवाः ॥
न प्रहष्येत् प्रियं प्राप्य नोद्विजेत् प्राप्य चाप्रियम् ।
स्थिरवुद्धिरसंमूढ़ो ब्रह्मविद् ब्रह्मणि स्थितः ॥
बाह्मस्पर्शेष्वसक्तात्मा विन्दत्यात्मनियत् सुखम् ।
स ब्रह्मयोगयुक्तात्मा सुखमद्मरयश्नुते ॥[31]

"Sages look equally on a Brahmana adorned with learning and humility, a cow, an elephant, and even a dog and an outcaste.

"Even here on earth they have conquered the universe whose mind remains balanced. Brahman is incorruptible and balanced; therefore they are established in Brahman.

"One should neither rejoice in obtaining what is pleasant,

30 *Bhagavad—Gita,* v, 10—12.

31 *Ibid,* v. 18—21.

nor sorrow in obtaining what is unpleasant; with Reason firm. unperplexed, the Brahman-knower (is) established in Brahman.

"He whose self is unattached to external contacts, and findeth joy in the Self, having the self harmonised with Brahman by yoga, enjoyeth happiness exempt from decay."

योऽन्तःसुखोऽन्तराणामस्तथान्तर्ज्योतिरेवयः ।
सयोगी ब्रह्मनिर्वाणां ब्रह्मभूतोऽधिगच्छति ॥
लभन्ते ब्रह्मनिर्वाणामृषयः क्षीणाकल्मषाः ।
छिन्नद्वैधायतात्मानः सर्वभूतहिते रताः ॥
कामक्रोधवियुक्तानांयतीनांयतचेतसाम् ।
श्रमितो ब्रह्मनिर्वाणां वर्तते विदितात्मनाम् ॥[32]

"He who is happy within, who rejoiceth within and who is illuminated within, that yogi, becoming Brahman, goeth to the Nirvana of Brahman.

"Rishis their sins destroyed, their duality removed, their selves controlled, intent upon the welfare of all beings, obtain the Nirvana of Brahman.

"The Nirvana of Brahman lies near to those who know themselves, who are disjoined from desire and passion, subdued ascetics, of controlled mind."

CHAPTER 4

KARMA

Karma is a Sanskrit word which means action, but it is generally used to mean a certain definite connection between what is being done now and what will happen in the future. Things do not

32 *Bhagavad-Gita*, v. 24-26.

happen by accident, by chance, in a disorderly way. They happen in regular succession; they follow each other in a regular order.

If a seed is planted in the ground, it sends up a little stem, and leaves grow on the stem and the flowers come, and then fruits, and in the fruits are seeds again. And one of these seeds planted will produce a stem, and leaves, and flowers and fruits and seeds. The same sort of seed produces the same kind of plants. Rice produces rice-plants; barley produces barley; wheat produces wheat; thistle produces thistle; cactus produces cactus. If a man sows thistles, he must not expect a crop of sweet grapes; if he plants prickly cactus, he must not expect to gather juicy apples. This is karma, and a man, knowing it, sows the seed of the thing he wants to reap. This is the first thing to remember.

Now an action is not quite so simple a thing as it looks. If I ask a person, "Why do you walk into the town?" he will say:" *I wanted* a pair shoes, and *I thought* I could get them there;" or: "*I wanted* to see a freind and *I thought* he was in the town;" and so on, in many ways, but always: "*I wanted* and *I thought* therefore *I acted.*" These three are always found together.

Now a *want* is what is called a desire; we *desire* to get somthing—that is the first stage; then we *think* how to get it—that is the second stage; then we *act* so as to get it—that is the third stage. This is the regular order; every action has a thought behind it and every thought has a desire behind it.

These three things—action, thought, desire—are the three threads that are twisted into the cord of karma. Our actions make the people round us happy or unhappy; if we make them happy, we have sown happiness like a seed, and it grows up into happiness for ourselves; if we make them unhappy, we have sown unhappiness like a seed, and it grows up into unhappiness for ourselves. If we do cruel things, we sow cruelty like a seed, and it grows up into cruelty to ourselves. If we do kind things, we sow kindness like a seed, and it grows up into kindness to ourselves. Whatever we sow by our actions comes back to us. This is karma.

But action has thought behind it. Now thought makes what is called our character, the nature and kind of mind that we have. As we think about a thing a great deal, our mind becomes like that thing. If we think kindly, we become kind; if we think cruelly, we become cruel; if we think deceitfully, we become deceitful; if we think honestly, we become honest. In this way our character is made by our thoughts, and when we are born again, we shall be born with the character that is being made by our thoughts now. As we act according to our nature, or character—as a kind person acts kindly, or a cruel person acts cruelly—it is easy to see that actions in our next life will depend on the thoughts of our present life. This is karma.

But thought has desire behind it. Now desire brings us the object we wish for. As a magnet attracts soft iron, so does desire attract objects. If we desire money, we shall have the opportunity of becoming rich in another life. If we desire learning, we shall have the opportunity of becoming learned in another life. If we desire love, we shall have the opportunity of becoming loved. If we desire power, we shall have the opportunity of becoming powerful. This is karma.

The student should think over this again and again till he thoroughly understands it. Only when he understands this, can he go on to the more difficult problems of karma. Karma may be summed up in a sentence: A man reaps as he sows.

But the student may ask: "If my actions now are the outcome of my past thoughts, and if my past thoughts are the outcome of my past desires, am I not helplessly bound? I must act as I have thought. I must think as I have desired." That is true, but to a certain extent only; for we are changing constantly as we gain new experiences, and the Jiva thus gains more knowledge, and by the help of that changes his desires. In other words, while we have *actually* desired, thought and acted in a certain way in the past, the *possibility* of desiring, of thinking *otherwise* has also been present throughout that past; and this possibility may be turned, at any time, into actuality, as soon as we realise, by means of new experiences, the evil consequences of acting as we have actually done in the past.

Suppose a man finds that he has acted cruelly: he learns that his cruel action was caused by his cruel thoughts in the past, and that those cruel thoughts grew out of desire to get an object which could only be obtained by cruelty. He sees that his cruel actions make people miserable, that these people hate and fear him, and thus make him lonely and unhappy. He thinks over all this, and he resolves to change, but the pressure of his past thoughts and desires is very difficult to resist. He goes to the root of the trouble—the desire for the things that he cannot get without cruelty, and he—who is the Jiva—says to himself: "I will not let myself desire those things, and whenever I begin to wish for them I will remember that the desire breeds misery." He uses thought to check desire, instead of letting desire control thought. Then instead of desires carrying him away, as if they were runaway horses, he gradually uses thought as a bridle, and keeps his desires in check. He will only allow them to run after objects that bring happiness when they are obtained.

Young Jivas let their desires run away with them, and so bring much unhappiness on them-selves; older Jivas grow wiser, and when the desire runs out to an object the possession of which would, as he has found in the past, cause unhappiness, he remembers that past unhappiness, and by his thought pulls the desire back.

The student, then, who would make happiness for others and for himself, must look well after his desires, must find out by observation and study which objects in the long run bring happiness, and which bring unhappiness, and must then try, with all his strength, to desire only those things the outcome of which is happiness.

It is very important to realise that escape from the bonds of birth and death is not gained by any special mode of life, but that, as Shri Krshna says: "He who, established in unity, worshippeth Me, abiding in all beings, that yogi liveth in Me, whatever his mode of living."[33] Janaka, the Kshattriya King and Tuladhara, the Vaishya merchant, equally reached liberation, and that, not by fleeing to the forest, but by the absence of desire for worldly things.

Janaka was King in Mithila, over the Videhas and, having attained to tranquility of mind, he sang this song: "Unlimited is my wealth, and yet I have naught. If the whole of Mithila be burned up with fire, yet for me there will be nothing lost."[34] And so he told Mandavya, having repeated this, that whatever possessions a man might have were but a source of trouble, and that the. gratification of desire, here or in heaven, could not afford the sixteenth part of the happiness which comes from the disappearance of desire. As the horns of a cow grow with the cow, so does the desire for wealth grow with its possession. Wealth should be used for the good that can be done with it, but desire is sorrow. Looking on all creatures as on himself, a wise man gains freedom from all anxiety.[35] By the teaching of the sage Jajnavalkya, King Janaka attained liberation, for it "enabled him to attain to that Brahman which is auspicious and immortal, and which transcends all sorrow."[36] And having thus learned, he became in his turn a teacher, to whom even Vyasa sent his son, Shuka, to learn the religion of emancipation.[37]

Jajali made great tapas, and became filled with pride; and one day he thought within himself: "who in this wide sea and spacious

---

33 B*hagavad-Gita,* vi.—31.

34 *Mahabharatam*. Shanti Parva, clxxiii.

35 *Mahabharatam*, cccxxvii.

36 See the great discourse of Yajnavalkya to King Janata; Ibid. Shanti Parva, cccxi—cacxix.

37 lbid, cccxxvi—cccxxviii.

earth is like to me?" Then cried a voice: "Say not such words. Even Tuladhara, busy in buying and selling, should not thus speak, and to him thou art not equal." Then Jajali wondered much that a mere merchant should be put above himself, a Brahmana and an ascetic, and he set forth to find Tuladhara, and thus solve the riddle. Vexing himself, he reached the city of Varanasi, and there found Tuladhara, a mere shopkeeper, selling, to whomsoever came, all kinds of goods. Tuladhara stood up, greeting the Brahmana as was fitting and to him Tuladhara related the story of the great penance that had inflated him with pride: "Angry, thou hast come to me, O Brahmana; what service can I render thee?" Much amazed was Jajali at such knowledge of his past shown by this humble trader, and eagerly he pressed for explanation. Then Tuladhara spoke to him of the ancient morality known to all—though practised by so few—of living in a way which inflicted harm on none, or when harm could not be totally avoided, a minimum of such harm; he himself asked no loan from any, nor with any quarrelled; attraction and aversion he had con quered; equal his look on ail, without praising or blaming any; when a man is fearless and is feared by none, when he neither likes nor dislikes, when he does no wrong to any, then he reaches Brahman. Very beautifully did Tuladhara discourse of the injuries inflicted on animals and on men by cruelty, of the nature of sacrifice, and of true pilgrimage, showing how liberation might be gained by harmlessness.[38]

काममय एवायं पुरुष इति सयथाकामो भवति तत्क्रतुर्भवति
यत्क्रतुर्भवति तत्कर्म कुरुते तत्कर्म कुरुते तदभिसम्पद्यते ॥[39]

"Man verily is desire-formed; as is his desire so is his thought; as (his) thought is, so he does action; as he does action, so he attains."

38 *Mahabharatam,* Shanti Parva, cclxi- cclxi.

39 Brihadaranyakop IV, iv—5.

तदेव सक्तः सह कर्मणैति लिङ्गं मनोयत्र निषक्तमस्य ।।[40]

"So indeed the desirer goes by work to the object in which his mind is immersed."

अथ खलु ऋतुमयः पुरुषोयथाकतुरस्मिँल्लोके पुरुषो भवति तथेतः
प्रेत्य भवति ।'[41]

"Now verily man is thought-formed; as man in this world thinks, so, having gone away hence, he becomes."

नमां कर्माणि लिम्पन्ति न मे कर्मफले स्पृहा ।
इति मांयोऽभिजानाति कर्मभिर्न स बध्यते ।।
एवं ज्ञात्वा कृतं कर्म पूर्वैरपि मुमुक्षुभिः ।
कुरु कर्मैव तस्मात् त्वं पूर्वैः पूर्वतरं कृतम् ।।[42]

"Nor do actions affect Me, nor is the fruit of action desired by Me. He who thus knoweth Me is not hound by actions."

"Having thus known, our forefathers, ever seeking liberation, performed action; therefore do thou also perform action, as did our forefathers in the olden time."

यस्य सर्वे समारम्भाः कामसंकल्पवर्जिताः ।
ज्ञानाग्निदग्धकर्माणां तमाहुः पणिडतं बुधाः ।।
त्यक्त्का कर्मफलासंगं नित्यतृप्तो निराश्रयः ।
कर्मरायभि प्रवृप्तोऽपि नैव किचिंत् करोति सः ।।
निराशीयंतचित्तात्मा त्यक्तसर्वपरिग्रहः ।
शारीरं केवल कर्म कुर्वन्नाप्नोति किल्विषम् ।।

40 Chhdndogyop. III, xiv—1.

41 Ibid, 6.

42 *Bhagavad-Gita*, , iv, 14—15

यदृच्छालाभसन्तुष्टो द्वन्द्वातीतो विमत्सरः ।
समः सिद्धावसिद्धौ च कृत्वापि न निवध्यंत॥
गतसंगस्य मुक्तस्य ज्ञानावस्थितचेतसः ।
यज्ञायाचरतः कर्म समग्रं प्रविलीयते ॥ 43

"Whose works are all free from the moulding of desire, whose actions are burned up by the fire of wisdom, him the wise have called a Sage."

''Having abandoned attachment to the fruit of action, always content, nowhere seeking refuge he is not doing anything, although doing actions.

"Hoping for naught, his mind and self controlled, having abandoned all greed, performing action by the body alone, he doth not commit sin."

"Of one with attachment dead, harmonious, with his thoughts established in wisdom, his works sacrifices, all action melts away."

यदा सर्वे प्रमुच्यन्ते कामायेऽस्य हृदि स्थिताः ।
त्र्प्रथ मर्त्योऽमृतो भवत्यत्र ब्रह्म समश्नुते ॥[44]

"When all the desires hidden in the heart are loosed, then the mortal becomes immortal, then he here enjoyeth Brahman."

आत्मानं रथिनं विद्धि शरीरं रथमेव तु ।
बुद्धिं तु सारर्थिं विद्धि मनः प्रग्रहमेवच ॥
इन्द्रियाणि हयानाहुर्विषयांस्तेषु गोचरान् ।
आत्मेन्द्रियमनोयुक्तं भोक्तेत्याहुर्मनीषिणाः ॥
यस्त्वविज्ञानवान् भवत्ययुक्तेन मनसा सदा ।
तस्येन्द्रियाण्यवश्यानि दुष्टाक्ष्वा इव सारथेः ॥

---

43 *Bhagavad-Gita*, , iv 19—23.

44 *Kathop*, II, vi—14

यस्तु विज्ञानवान्भवतियुक्तेन मनसा सदा ।
तस्येन्द्रियाणिा वश्यानि सदक्ष्वा इव सारथेः ॥
यस्त्वविज्ञानवान्भवत्यमनस्कः सदाऽशुचिः ।
न स तत्पदमाप्रोति संसारं चाधिगच्छति ॥[45]

"Know the Self, the chariot-owner, the body, the chariot; know Reason the charioteer, and the mind as the reins; they call the senses the horses, the sense-objects their province. The Self, joined to the senses and mind, (is) the enjoyer; thus say the wise. Whoever is ignorant, always with mind lose, his senses (are) uncontrolled, like bad horses of the charioteer. Whoever is wise, always with mind tightened, his senses (are) controlled, like good horses of the charioteer. Whoever is indeed ignorant, thoughtless, always impure, he does not obtain that goal (but) comes again into Samsara."

CHAPTER 5

SACRIFICE

The idea of "offering sacrifices" is very familiar in India, but a student needs to understand the principle which underlies all sacrifices, so that he may realise that every one should sacrifice *himself* to the good of others, and that all sacrifice of other things are meant, to teach a man how he ought, at last, to sacrifice himself.

The Law of Sacrifice is the Law of Life for all Jivas. In the earlier stages of their growth they are forcibly sacrificed, and so progress involuntarily, without their own consent or even knowledge, their forms being violently wrenched away from them, and they propelled into new ones, a little more developed. Thus the Jivas of the mineral kingdom are prepared to pass on into the vegetable, by the breaking up of their mineral bodies for the support

45 *Kathop,* I, iii, 3—7.

of plants. The Jivas of the vegetable kingdom are prepared to pass on into the animals, by the breaking up of their vegetable bodies for the support of animal life. The Jivas of the animal kingdom are prepared to pass on into the human, by the breaking up of their bodies for the support of other animals, of savages, and of certain types of men. And even the Jivas of the human kingdom are prepared to rise into higher races by breaking up of their human bodies for the support of other human lives in cannibalism, war, etc.

In all these cases the bodies are sacrificed for the benefit of others, without the assent of the embodied consciousness. Only after untold ages does the Jiva recognise, in the body, the universality of the law, and begin to sacrifice his own upadhis deliberately, for the good of those around him. This is called self-sacrifice, and is the showing forth of the divinity of the Jiva, the proof that he is of the nature of Ishvara.

A wonderful story of uttermost self-sacrifice is told in the *Mahabharatam.*

Indra, the King of the Devas, was sore beset by the Asura Vrittra, born of the wrath of a Rishi, whom Indra had offended by an unrighteous act. Vrittra heading the Daityas, defeated Indra and his armies in battle, drove him away from his capital, Amaravati and took away his sovereignty. Long the Devas wandered with their King in exile, and repeatedly they made endeavour to regain their capital, but were vanquished again and again. Finally they learnt that the righteous wrath of a Rishi could not be allayed, except by the voluntary self-sacrifice and pity of another Rishi; and that Vrittra could be slain by no other weapon than the thunderbolt made with the self-given bones of a holy one. And they went eagerly to the Rishi Dadhichi and told their woeful tale to him. And he was filled with a geat pity and said: "I give to you my body willingly to make what use of it you like." And when their artificer Vishvakarma shrank from laying a rude and painful hand upon that shining body of purity and tapas, Dadhichi smiled and said: "Cover this body up with salt; bring here a herd of cows; they shall lick off the salt and flesh together; and ye shall take the bones which only ye require; and so naught of this body shall be wasted." And this was done and Vrittra fell before the might born of that wondrous sacrifice.[46]

The Jiva is led up to this point by the teachings of the Rishis, who bid him make sacrifices of his possessions for a good that he does not receive immediately: they show him that when a man sacrifices to others, his gifts return to him increased in the future. A man is to sacrifice some of his goods, which may be looked on as outlying pieces of himself, and he is promised that this act of self-denial shall bring him increased possessions. Next he was taught to make similar sacrifices and to deny himself present enjoyments, in order that he might lay up for himself increased happiness on the other side of death in Svarga. Thus the practice of sacrificing was made habitual, and man, by sacrificing his possessions in the hope of reward, prepared to learn that it was his duty to sacrifice himself in the service of others, and to find in the joy of that service his reward.

Another lesson taught in these sacrifices was the relation man bears to all the beings round him; that he is not a solitary, isolated life, but that all lives are inter-dependent, and can only prosper permanently as they recognise this inter-dependence. The Rishis taught him to sacrifice daily to the Devas, to Rishis, to ancestors, to men and animals, and showed him that as all these made sacrifices to enrich his life, he had incurred to them a debt, a duty, which he must pay by sacrifice. As he lives *on* others, he must, in common honesty, live *for* others. Sacrifice is right, a thing that ought to be done, that is owed.

Finally, as the Jiva recognises his parentage, his identity in nature with Ishvara, sacrifice becomes happiness, a delight, and the pouring out of life for others is felt as a joyous exercise of

---

46 Loc. cit, Vana Prava, c.

innate divine powers. Instead of seeing how much he can take and how little he can give, he tries to see how little he. can take and how much he can give. He begins to look very carefully into what he takes for the support of his own upadhis, and seeks to reduce to the lowest point the suffering inflicted by the breaking up of lower forms for his support. He abandons the foods and the amusements which inflict pain on sentient beings and tries to become "the friend of all creatures.' He realises that while the preying of animals on animals, of men on men, and the slaughter of animals by men for food or sport, are necessary at certain stages of evolution for the development of needed faculties and powers, men should gradually evolve from these, and cultivate the faculties of gentleness, sympathy and tenderness, regarding the weaker as younger Selves to be helped, instead of as victims to be immolated.

As a man lives in such thoughts of his nonseparateness from younger Selves, he begins to feel more really his non-separateness from elder Selves and from the Universal Parent, Ishvara. Slowly he realises that his true function is to live for others, as Ishvara lives for all, and that his true happiness lies in becoming a channel in which the life of Ishvara is flowing, a willing instrument to do the will of Ishvara. Then every action becomes a sacrifice to Ishvara, and actions no longer bind him. Thus the law of sacrifice becomes also the law of liberation.

सहयज्ञैः प्रजाः सृष्टाः पुरोवाच प्रजापतिः ।
अनेन प्रसविष्यध्वं एष वो ऽस्त्विष्टकामधुक् ॥
देवान् भावयतानेन ते देवा भावयन्तु वः।
परस्पंर भावयन्तः श्रेयः परमवाप्स्यथ ॥
इष्टान् भोगान् हि वो देवा दास्यन्तेयज्ञभाविताः ।
तैर्दत्तानप्रदायैभ्योयो भुङ्क्तेस्तेन एव सः ॥
यज्ञशिष्टाशिनः सन्तो मुच्यन्ते सर्वकिल्बिषैः ।

भुञ्जते ते त्वघं पापाये पचन्त्यात्मकारणात् ॥
अन्नाद् भवन्ति भूतानि पर्जन्यादन्नसम्भवः ।
यज्ञाद् भवति पर्जन्योयशः कर्मसमुन्द्रवः ॥
कर्मब्रह्मोद्भवं विद्धि ब्रह्मक्षरसमुद्भवम् ।
तस्मात् सर्वगतं ब्रह्म नित्यंयज्ञे प्रतिष्ठितम् ॥[47]

"Having in ancient times emanated mankind together with sacrifice, Prajapati declared: 'By this shall ye propagate; be this to you the Kamadhuk:

"With this nourish ye the Devas, and may the Devas nourish you; thus nourishing one another ye shall reap the supremest good.

"For, nourished by sacrifice, the Devas, shall bestow on you the enjoyments you desire. A thief verily is he who enjoyeth what is given by them without returning them aught.

''The righteous, who eat the remains of the sacrifice, are freed from all sins; but the impious, who dress food for their own sakes, they verily eat sin.

"From food creatures come forth; from rain is the production of food; rain proceedeth from sacrifice; sacrifice ariseth out of action.

"Know thou from Brahma (the Veda) action groweth, and Brahma (the Veda) from the Imperishable, cometh. Therefore Brahman, the all permeating, is ever present in sacrifice.'"

काङ्क्षन्तः कर्मणां सिद्धि अजन्त इह देवताः ।
क्षिप्रं हि मांनुषे लोके सिद्धिर्भवति कर्मजा ॥[48]

"They who long after success in action on earth sacrifice to the Devas; for in brief space, verily, in this world of men, success is born of action."

---

47 *Bhagavad-Gita,* iii, 10— 15.

48 *Bhagavad-Gita*, iv, 12

आवां राजानावध्वरे ववृत्यां हव्येभिरिन्द्रावरुणा नमोभिः ।
अस्मे इन्द्रावरुणा विश्ववारं रयिं धक्षं वसुयन्तं पुरुक्षुम् ॥
इयमिन्द्रं वरुणामष्टमे गीः प्रावत्तांके तनके तूतुजाना ।[49]

"O Kings, Indra, Yaruna, to this our sacrifice be ye turned by offerings and homage,......

"O Indra, Varuna, plenteous wealth and food and blessing give us......

"This my song may it reach Indra, Varuna, and by its force bring sons and offspring.

एतेषुयश्चरते भ्राजमानेषु
यथाकालं चाहुतयो ह्यददायन् ।
तन्नयन्त्येतः सूर्यस्य रश्मयो–
यत्र देवानां पतिरेकोऽधिवासः ॥
एह्येहोति तमाहुतयः सुवर्चसः
सूर्यस्य रश्मिभिर्यजमानं वहन्ति ।
प्रियां वाचमभिवदन्त्योऽर्चयन्त्य
एष वः पुरायः सुकृतो ब्रह्मलोकः ॥[50]

"Whoever works (sacrifices), pouring libations into the shining of these [the seven flames previously mentioned] at the proper time, him these sun-rays lead where dwells the one Lord of the Devas. Saying to him ' Come, come,' these resplendent libations carry the sacrificer by the sun-rays, worshipping him and saying the sweet words:

यज्ञशिष्टामृंतभुजोयान्ति ब्रंह्म सनातनम् ।
नायं लोकोऽस्त्यंयज्ञस्य कुतोऽन्यः कुरुसत्तम ॥[51]

49 Rigveda, VII, lxxxiv, I, 4—5.

50 *Mundakop.* I. ii„ 5—6

51 *Bhagavad-Gita,* iv—31.

"The eaters of the life-giving remains of sacrifice go to the eternal Brahman. This world is not for the non-saerificer, much less the other, O best of the Kurus. "

गतसंगस्य मुक्तस्य ज्ञानावस्थितचेतसः ।
यज्ञायाचरतः कर्म समग्रं प्रविलीयते ॥[52]

"From one with attachment dead, harmonious, with his thoughts established in wisdom, his works sacrifices, all Karma melts away.

यत्करोषियदश्नासियज्जुहोषि ददासियत् ।
यत्तपस्यसि कौन्तेय तत्कुरुष्वं मदर्पणाम् ॥
शुभाशुभफलैरंव मोक्ष्यसे कर्मबन्धनैः ।[53]

"Whatsoever thou doest, whatsoever thou eatest, whatsoever thou offerest, whatsoever thou givest, whatsoever thou doest of austerity, O Kaunteya, do thou that as an offering unto me.

"Thus shalt thou be liberated from the bonds of action, (yielding) good and evil fruits."

CHAPTER 6

THE WORLDS—VISIBLE AND INVISIBLE

We all know one world, the world around us, which we can see, and hear, and touch, and taste, and smell. Science tells us of many parts of this world, which our senses are not keen enough to perceive, things too small for our eyes to see, too subtle to affect any of our senses. These parts of our world, which we

52 *Ibid*, 23.

53 *Ibid*, ix, 27- 28.

cannot perceive but about which science tells us, are still physical, although invisible to us; they are parts of our world. Physical matter includes solids, liquids, gases, and ethers, all made up of atoms of the same kind.

But we have heard of other worlds, which are invisible and are not a part of this world, the worlds into which people go when they pass away from this earth by death. We read of the Triloka, the three worlds, and every one should know something about these, for in these three worlds the Jiva is bound to the wheel of births and deaths, and in these his evolution proceeds. These three worlds are made at the beginning of immense period called a Day of Brahma, and perish at its ending. Four other great lokas, or worlds, complete the Brahmanda, but they last on through the life of Brahma. We need not deal with them here. There are also some sub-divisions within the great lokas, to which the same name of loka is given, such as, Pretaloka and Pitriloka in Bhuvarloka, and Indraloka and Suryaloka in Svargaloka.

The three great lokas with which we are concerned, the Triloki, are: Bhurloka, the physical world, or the earth; Bhuvarloka, the world of "becoming"—intermediate between the earth and Svarga; Svargaloka, the heaven world. Of these three, Bhurloka is partly visible and partly invisible to us; Bhuvarloka and Svargaloka are invisible. In Bhurloka the Prithvi Tattva is the basis of all forms: it exists in seven modifications—solid, liquid, gaseous, radiant, etheric, superetheric and atomic. These later four are spoken as "the ethers." In Bhuvarloka seven similar modifications exist, but the basis is the Apas Tattva. In Svargaloka there are also seven similar modifications, but the basis is the Agni Tattva.

The Jiva has three sheaths corresponding to these worlds—the Annamayakosha, the Pranamayaskosha, the Manomayakosha. The Annamayakosha, or food-sheath—so called because it is built up out of the food we eat—corresponds with the visible part of the earth and is composed of solids, liquids and gases. The Pranamayakosha or Prana-sheath, corresponds with the invisible part of our earth and is composed of ethers. Prana is the life-energy, and includes all the forces that science calls magnetic and electrical, but is much more than these. Both these sheaths are connected with Bhurloka.

The Manomayakosha, mind-sheath, has two parts; the denser part, in which the passions have their seat, is connected with Bhuvarloka; the liner part, in which play the emotions and thought, is connected with Svargaloka.

Other names are used for these sheaths, according to the object for which the classification is made, but the student need not become confused by these, for as he advances, he will find that his increased knowledge makes them quite intelligible. We will only notice three names very commonly used.

The sthulasharira, or solid body, is the same as the Annamayakosha, made of solids, liquids and gases. The Sukshmasharira, or subtle body, includes the Pranamayakosha and the Manomayakosha; in addition to these, it includes another kosha, the Vijnanamayakosha, the knowledge sheath, which connects the Jiva with muharloka, a loka beyond the Triloka in which his pilgrimage is carried on, one which is not destroyed, though it is rendered uninhabitable, at the close of the Day of Brahma. This part of the Sukshmasharira. the knowledge-sheath, is relatively permanent, and lasts through the series of births and deaths.

A table may make these two classifications, and their relation to the lokas, clear:—

Sharira.	Loka.	Kosha.
Sthula.	Bhurloka.	Annamaya.
Sukshma.	Bhurloka.	Pranamaya.
Sukshma	Bhuvarloka.	Manomaya.
Sukshma.	Svargaloka.	Manomaya.

[These perish at or after death and are renewed at re-birth.]

Sukshma (Karana) Maharloka. Vijnanamaya.

[This does not perish at or after death, so is not renewed at re-birth.]

The Sthulasharira contains the *organs* of action, the hands, feet and those of speech, generation and excretion, often called the Karmendriyas; but the true Karmendriyas, *the centres which direct and control the organs*, are in the Sukshmasharira. Thus joy, or grief, or any strong emotion, affects the centres, and through them, the organs; the hands twitch, the feet tap, speech is impeded in irritation, and so on The Jnanendriyas have also their centres in the Sukshmasharira. while their organs—eyes, ears, tongue, nose and skin—are in the Sthulasharira.

Now let us see what happens at death. First, the Sukshmasharira is separated from the Sthulasharira, the Jiva drawing it away by means of the Pranamayakosha. This leaves the Sthulasharira a mass of "lifeless" matter; that is, of matter from which the life that held it together is withdrawn; there is plenty of life left in the cells of the body, and they begin to break aw ay from each other, but the ruling life is gone. The Jiva remains in his Sukshmasharira. Very quickly he shakes off his Prunamayakosha, and has then the denser part of the Manomayakosha as bis outer-most garment. He is then called a Preta, and is an inhabitant of Pretaloka. If he has been a very good man on earth, he dreams away happily while in this condition; but if he has been a bad man, he suffers while a Preta, craving for the earthly pleasures which he is no longer able to obtain. After a shorter or longer time—according to the strength of these cravings and the consequent length of time needed for their exhaustion—the densest part of the. Manomayakosha falls away, and he goes as a Pitri into Pitriloka. Having spent there sufficient time to purify the Manomayakosha from all elements unlit for Svarga, the Jiva in the purified Manomayakosha goes on into Svarga, and enjoys there the fruit he has stored up.

When this is exhausted, the time has come for his return to earth, and the purified Manomayakosha dissolves away, leaving the Jiva in the Vijnanamayakosha. He quickly puts forth his power to form new vehicles, and creates a new Manomayakosha for his coming life in the lower worlds. The Devas build for him a Pranamayakosha and an Annamayakosha, according to his karma, and he is again born into Bhurloka.

These are the recurring stages of the Jiva's pilgrimage: life in the visible world, death, life in the invisible worlds, re-birth. This is repeated time after time, time after time. At last, the Jiva grows weary of these three worlds, and longs for higher, subtler experiences and more expanded life; he turns away from all these worlds can offer him, and finds delight in meditation, in worship, in the compassionate helping of the weaker; he no longer uses his vehicles to gain pleasure for himself, but only to do service to others, and, so used, they can no longer imprison him, He dwells in the higher lokas, guiding his lower vehicles as his instruments in the lower worlds, and becomes a co-worker with Ishvara, either retaining his vehicles for service or throwing them away and entering into Brahman.

अथ त्रयो वाव लोकामनुष्यलोकः पितृलोको देवलोक इति ।[54]

"Now verily there are three worlds—the world of men, the world of the Pitris, the world of the Devas."

जातस्य हि ध्रुवो मृत्युर्ध्रुवं जन्म मृतस्य च ।
तस्मादपरिहार्येऽर्थे न त्वं शोचितुमर्हसि ॥
अव्यक्तादीनि भूतानि व्यक्तमध्यानि भारत ।
अव्यक्तनिधनान्येव तत्र का परिदेवना ॥[55]

---

54 *Brihadaranyakop.* I, v–16,

55 *Bhagavad-Gita,* ii; 27–28.

"For certain is death for the born, and certain is birth for the dead; therefore over the inevitable thou shouldst not grieve.

"Beings are unmanifest in their origin, manifest in their midmost state, O Bharata, unmanifest in their dissolution: what room then for lamentation?

सहस्त्रयुगपर्यन्तमहर्यद् ब्रह्मणो विदुः ।
रात्रियुगसहस्त्रान्तां तेऽहोरात्रविंदो जनाः ॥
श्रव्यक्ताद्व्यक्तयः सर्वाः प्रभवन्त्यहरागमे ।
रात्र्यागमे प्रलीयन्ते तत्रैवाव्यक्तसंज्ञके ॥[56]

"The pople who know the Day of Brahma, a thousand Yugas in duration, and the Night, a thousand Yugas in ending, they know day and night.

"From the unmanifested all the manifested stream forth at the coming of Day; at the coming of Night they dissolve, even in that called the unmanifested."

त्रैविद्या मां सोमपाः पूतपापाः
यज्ञैरिष्ट्र स्वर्गतिं प्रार्थयन्ते ।
ते पुरायमाससाद्य सुरेंद्रलोक–
मश्नन्ति दिव्यान्दिवि देवभोगान्
ते तं भुक्त्वा स्वर्गलोकं विशालं
क्षीणो पुराये मर्त्यलोकं विशन्ति ।
एवं त्रयीधर्ममनुप्रपन्ना
गतागतं कामकामा लभन्ते ॥[57]

"The knowers of the three (Veda), the Soma drinkers, the purified from sin, worshipping Me with sacrifice, pray of Me the

56 *lbid* viii; 17—18.

57 *Bhagavad-Gita,* ix, 20- 21.

way to Svarga; they ascending to the holy word of the Deva Indra, enjoy in heaven the divine feasts of the Devas.

"Having enjoyed the spacious Svarga-world, their holiness withered, they come back to this world of death. Following the virtues enjoined by the three (Vedas), desiring desires, they undergo this passage to and fro."

बहूनां जन्मनामन्ते ज्ञानवान्मां प्रपद्यते ।
वासुदेवः सर्वमिति स महात्मा सुदुर्लभः ॥[58]

"At the end of many births the man full of wisdom cometh unto me: ' Vasudeva is all,' saith he, the Mahatma, very difficult to find."

58 *Ibid*. vii, 19.

PART II

GENERAL HINDU RELIGIOUS CUSTOMS AND RITES

CHAPTER I

THE SAMSKARAS

Every religion prescribes a number of ceremonies, or rites, to be performed by its followers. The use of the ceremonies, speaking generally, is: (1) to help the Jiva to conquer and purify his sheaths; (2) to bring to his aid superior Intelligences, such as the Devas and the Rishis; (3) to improve the atmosphere around him and so make it easier for him to steady and concentrate his mind.

To this end are used material objects, gestures, postures and sounds, all carefully arranged to bring about the results aimed at.

The objects used are chosen for their good magnetism, and in many cases—such as particular flowers offered to a particular Deva—because they share the magnetism of the Object of meditation or of worship, and thus make a link between that Object and the worshipper. Thus a mala. a rosary, of tulasi beads is used in the worship of Shri Krishna; one of rudritksha in the worship of Mahadeva.

Gestures and postures, for the most part, affect the Pranas—the sub-divisions of the life-breath that circulate in the body; some prevent the magnetism of the body from escaping into the surrounding atmosphere, and force its currents to move in a way suitable for calm and quiet thought.

Sounds are used for all the three purposes mentioned above. They give rise to vibrations, and as these vibrations are regular and even, they make the vibrations of the Sukshmasharira—which is very sensitive and easily affected—regular and even also. When these vibrations of the Sukshmasharira are made regular, the Jiva is much helped in steadiness of thought and devotion. Sounds of a suitable kind attract the attention of the Rishis and Devas to the person uttering the sounds, and they help him. Further, suitable sounds drive away hostile Intelligences and bad magnetic influences, and so improve the, surroundings of the speaker.

Sounds thus used are called Mantras. A mantra is a succession of sounds, a definite sequence, the sounds being arranged in a certain order: if the sounds are changed the vibrations are changed, and the results will be changed. That is why a mantra cannot be translated. A translated mantra is like a sentence in which all the letters of the words are jumbled up. and so convey no meaning.

There is another thing to remember about mantra; If the man who utters a mantra is not trying to lead a good life, the vibrations of the mantra will do him harm, not good. For, as they work on his Sukshmasharira, they bring to bear on it a force antagonistic to evil desires and evil thoughts, and shake it very violently and may even wound and tear it, as his evil resolves make it vibrate in one way and the vibrations of the mantra force it into another. If his resolves are good then they work with the mantra and cause no conflict; however weak they may be. they aid and do not hinder.

Mantras need not be spoken aloud, and their silent repetition is, indeed, more powerful than audible recitation. They affect the subtler kinds of matter more than the denser.

Among the ceremonies in the life of a Hindu are some important ones that mark the chief stages of his life; in old days these were numerous, ten standing out as the chief, but of these ten, only some are. now practised. Seven of the Samskaras relate to infantile life and early childhood. Of these seven, the sixth, Annaprasanam, the first feeding with solid food, is universally observed; and the seventh, Chudakaranam—the tonsure, and with it the piercing of the ears—is performed almost universally. Then comes the important eighth Samskara, the Upanayana, the leading of the boy to the Guru who gives him the sacred thread, and teaches him the Gayatri, this initiation making him a Dvija, twice-born.

The Upanayana is the beginning of the student stage of life, during which Brahmacharya, entire celibacy, is enjoined, and the duty of the lad is to study diligently. This stage is closed by the formal return home, the Samavartanam, after which he is ready to enter the second stage of life, that of the householder, the Grihastha; the tenth Samskara, Vivaha, marriage, marking his entry into manhood and its responsibilities. In modern India these wholesome rules have fallen into disuse, though the Upanayana and Vivaha Samskaras are maintained as ceremonies. Marriage is incongruously thrust into the midst of the student life, and the duties of manhood and boyhood are mixed up to the injury of both. May the ancient rule be speedily revived.

एकः शब्दः सुप्रयुक्तः स्वर्गे लोके कामधुग्भवति ।[59]

"One sound, well-uttered, becometh as the cow of plenty in the Svarga-world."

मंत्रो हीनः स्वरतो वर्णातो वा
मिथ्या प्रयुक्तो न तमर्थमाह ।
स वाग्वज्रोयजमानं हिनस्ति
यथेन्द्रशत्रुः स्वरतोऽपराधात् ॥[60]

"The mantra defective in Svara (inflection) or Varna (letter or colour) is uttered falsely and declared not the true meaning. That lightning-word slayeth the performer himself as (the word) 'Indra-Shatru' for fault of Svara (slew Vrittra, the performer of

59 *Patanjali's* Mahabhasbya, vi, i—84.

60 *Panini-Shiksha,* 52.

the sacrifice, and the enemy of Indra, instead of slaying Indra, the enemy of Vrittra, as intended).

वैदिकैः कर्माभिः पुरायैर्निषकोदिर्द्विजन्मनाम्
कार्यः शरीरसंस्कारः पावनः प्रेत्य चेह च ॥[61]

"With sacred Vaidika rites should be performed the Samskaras of the body, namely, Nisheka and the rest, of the twice-born, which purify here and hereafter."

चित्रकर्मयथाऽनेकैरागैरुन्मल्यिते शनैः ।
ब्राह्मरायमपि तद्वत्स्यात्संस्कारैर्विधिपूर्वकैः ॥[62]

"As the outline of a picture is lighted up slowly with (the filling in of) many colours, even so is Bruhmanya with scriptural Samskaras."

गर्भाधानं पुंसवनं सीमंतो जातकर्म च ।
नामक्रिया निष्क्रमोऽन्नप्राशनं वपनक्रिया ॥
कर्णविधो व्रतादेशी वेदारम्भक्रियाविधिः ।
केशांतः स्नानमुद्वाहो विवाहाग्निपरिग्रहः ॥
त्रेताग्निसंग्रहश्चैव संस्काराः षोडश स्मृताः ।[63]

61 *Manusmriti,* ii—26.

62 *Angira* quoted in *Parashara-Grihya-Sutra, Hariara bhashya,* p. 260. (II. i.)

63 *Vyasa-Smriti* quoted in *Parashara Grihya-Sutra*, p. 269.

CHAPTER 2

SHRADDHA

Shraddha is the name of the ceremonies performed to help the Jiva, who has put off bis visible body in death, by those who remain in this world. The Jiva that has put off his visible body is called a Preta, and the part of the Shraddha performed to help him at this stage is called the Preta-kriya. The visible body, the Annumayakosha, is carried to the burning-ground that it may be dissolved into its constituents as quickly as possible; the ashes are gathered together on the third day, and are thrown into running water, preferably into a sacred stream. When the Annamayakosha is destroyed, the Pranamayakosha rapidly disperses, and this dispersal is quickened by some of the mantras used at the cremation. Burning is the best way of destroying a dead body, and this destruction is important both for the departed Jiva and for those left behind; so long as it remains undissolved, the Pranamayakosha hangs round it, in consequence of the magnetic attraction between them, and the Jiva is thus linked to the earth, which is bad for him; on the other hand, a slowly decaying body in the ground, as in burial, semis out poisonous gases, and this is bad for those remaining behind.

The Shraddhas performed after the burning help in a re-arrangement of the materials of the Manomayakosha. partly by the magnetic influences of the objects used, and partly by the vibrations set up by the mantras. After a certain time, the Sapindikarana ceremony is performed, which helps the Jiva to pass from Pretaloka, to Pitriloka, and he is then enrolled among the Pitris, or the ancestors living in the subtler regions of Bhuvarloka. Seven generations, one in Bhurloka and six in Bhuvarloka. can affect each other. When the Jiva passes on into Svarga, he has no further need of the help furnished by Shraddha.

देशे काले च पात्रे च श्रद्धया विधिना चयत् ।
पितृनुद्दिश्य विप्रेभ्यो दानं श्राद्धमुदाहृतम् ॥[64]

"Gifts to deserving Brahmanas for the sake of benefit to the Pitris, in the proper times and places and with faith, are known as Shraddha."

कुर्यादहरहः श्राद्धमन्नाद्येनोदकेन च ।
पयामूलफलैर्वापि पितृभ्यः प्रीतिमावहन् ॥[65]

"Shraddha should be offered to the Pitris. day by day, with corn and water, or even roots and fruits and water, bringing them satisfaction."

पंचक्ष्य एव मात्राभ्यः प्रेत्य दुष्कृतिनां नृणाम् ।
शरीरंयातनार्थीयमन्यदुत्पद्यते ध्रुवम् ॥
तेनानुभूय तायामीः शरीरेणोहयातनाः ।
तास्वेव भूतमात्रासु प्रलीयन्ते विभागशः ।
तैरेव चावृतो भूतैः स्वर्गे सुखमुपाश्नुते ॥[66]

"Out of the five elements a (subtler but) firm body is born (as seeth) for sinful Jivas (after death), that they may suffer punishment therein.

"After the suffering of the punishments awarded by Yama, in that body (the body) dissolves again into the elements.

---

64 Br*ahmanda Purana,*

65 *Manusmriti*. iii—203.

66 Ma*nusmriti,* xii, 16, 17, 20,

"If (the Jiva) has done more Dharma and little Adharma. he goes bn to Svarga and enjoys happiness there enclosed in (another body composed of) the same elements."

चितामोक्षप्रभृति च प्रेतत्वमुपजायते ।[67]

"After the cremation is completed (the Jiva) becomes a Preta."

वंर्षयावत् खगश्रेष्ठ ! मार्गो गच्छति मानवः ।
ततः पितृगणौः सार्धे पितृलोकं स गच्छति ॥
दत्तैः षोडशभिः श्राद्धैः पितृभिः सह मोदते ।
पितुः पुत्रेणा कर्तव्यं सर्पिडीकरणां सदा ॥[68]

"The Jiva remains on the path (*i e.,* the Pretaloka) for a year, O best of birds; then he passes on into the Pitri-loka (and dwells) with the Pitris.

"By the offering of the sixteen Shraddhas he is helped to dwell in joy with the Pitris. Therefore should the son ever perform the Sapindikarana rites for the father."

CHAPTER 3

SHAUCHAM

Shaucham, or Shaucha, consists of the rules laid down for keeping bodily purity, and thus ensuring physical health and strength. Disease is a sign that some law of nature has been disregarded, and the Rishis—knowing that the laws of nature are the laws of God, the expression of His being, and that the Jiva is a portion of God

67 *Garuda Purana,* II, t—36.

68 *Ibid*, II, ivi—6, 7, 20.

enveloped in matter—have treated obedience to the laws of nature as a religious duty.

The visible body, with its invisible double, the Pranamayakosha, being made of physical materials, it is necessary to use physical means to make them pure, and to keep them pure, and we need to understand them in order to do this.

The visible body, the Annamayakosha, is composed of particles drawn from the food we eat, the liquids we drink, the air we breathe, and from a constant rain of minute particles, too tiny for us to see, that falls upon us continually from the people and the things around us. This last statement may sound a little strange, but it is true. Our bodies are not made of dead matter, for there is no such thing as dead matter.[69] Matter is made of tiny living things called atoms, and of other tiny living things that are collections of atoms. A grain of dust is a collection of myriads upon myriads of tiny living creatures, and there are grades upon grades of these minute lives, till we come to what are called microbes, that can be seen with the help of microscopes. Now these microbes and the other smaller lives are all floating about in the air, and our bodies and all things are made up of these. Stones, plants, animals, human beings and all the manufactured things round us, houses, furniture, clothes are constantly giving off clouds of these particles. Everything near us, and still more, everything we touch, gives us some of its particles and we give it some of ours. If we are to be healthy, we must only take into our bodies pure particles and drive away impure ones. The rules of Shaucha are intended to show us how to do this.

The food we eat must he pure. Now all things are becoming more alive, or are getting nearedeath; are being built up, or are being destroyed. Pure food is becoming more alive, has life in it which is unfolding: its next natural stage is one of "higher integration,"

69 See p. 67. for what is meant by lifeless matter. A body, as a whole, is said to be "dead when the Jiva has left it. although the particles of it arc alive. As this "dead body" decays, the living particles are set free.

that is, of greater complexity. Fresh leaves and fruits, grains and roots, are full of life which is unfolding; we take that life into our bodies, and it builds them up. These things become impure if they are stale, for the life is then departing, they are on the way to death. All flesh is more or less impure, because its indwelling life has been driven from it, and it is ready to decay; its next natural stage is one of "disintegration," that is, of breaking up into simpler forms; the body built by it is more liable to disease than the body built of plant-products, wounds heal less quickly, and fevers run higher.

Of liquids, pure water is necessary to health, and infusions of herbs in it, such as tea, coffee and cocoa, taken in moderation, are harmless and often useful. Milk is at once food and drink of the purest kind. Every form of drink into which alcohol enters is impure, and most harmful to the body. It is fermented liquor, that is liquor in which decomposition has begun, and it injures the tissues of the body, and is a distinct poison to the brain. Especially it is mischievous in a hot climate, bringing about premature decay and early death. So also are drinks impure into which enter such stupefying drugs as Indian hemp—the popular but health destroying bhang.

Pure air is as necessary to health as pure food and drink. As we breathe, we send out a gas, called carbon dioxide, which is stupefying, and if we shut ourselves into a confined space, all the air in it becomes laden with this, and unfit to breathe. Further the breath carries out with it waste particles from the interior of the body, and unless the fresh air blows these away, they are breathed in again into our lungs and those of others, and are poisonous in their effects.

We must not only build up our bodies out of clean materials, but we must keep the surface of the body clean by frequent washing and bathing. The whole body must be bathed, at least once everyday, and well rubbed in bathing, so that all loose particles may be washed away, and the skin kept clean and fresh. Any part of the body that becomes soiled, feet, hands, etc., should be washed and washing before and after food must never be omitted. To eat with unwashed hands is to run the risk of soiling the food with dust and other injurious particles, and the washing after food is obviously imperative. The garments next the body should also be washed daily.

The Hindu, ever accustomed to look at the outer world as the symbol of the inner, has joined to his outer ablutions the idea of inner purification. As he washes the outer body, he repeats mantras for the purifying of the inner bodies, and thus weaves his religion into the commonest incidents of daily life.

Students will now see why the Rishis were so particular about cleanliness. A person with a dirty body, or with dirty clothes, fills the air round him with impure particles, and poisons the people round him. We must be clean, not only for our own sakes, but for the sake of those around us. A dirty person, dirty clothes, dirty houses, are centres of poison, public dangers.

The purity of the Pranamayakosha depends on the magnetic currents in it. It is quickly affected by the magnetic properties of surrounding objects, and we have therefore to be careful on this point also. Thus some plant-products and plants, while harmless to the Annamayakosha, are very injurious to the Pranamayakosha, such as onions and garlic. Their magnetism is worse than that of flesh. This kosha is also most seriously affected by alcoholic emanations, and by the Pranamayakoshas of others. What is still more important is that it is affected by its own Manomayakosha and, through it, by those of others. Hence the dangers of bad company. Now the purity of the Manomayakosha depends on the purity of its owner's thoughts and desires, and herein lies the most fertile source of impurity in the Annamaya and Pranamayakoshas. These two physical koshas cannot be pure and healthy if the thoughts and desires are impure. A man may observe the rules of Shaucha to the last point of strictness, hut if he be proud, passionate, harsh, vain, suspicious, he is pouring impurity into these koshas faster than any rules can wash it out. In the eyes of the Rishis and the Devas such a one is ever ashuchi.

दूरादावसथान्मूत्रं दूरात् पादावसेचनम् ।
उच्छिष्टान्नं निषेकं व दूरादेव समाचरेत् ॥[70]

"Far from his dwelling let him remove excrement, far the water used for washing his feet, far the leavings of food, and bath water."

श्राचस्य प्रयतो नित्यमुभे संध्ये समाहितः ।
शुचौ देशे जपञ्जप्यमुपासीतयथाविधि ॥[71]

"Being purified by sipping water, he shall always daily worship in the two twilights with a collected mind, in a pure place, performing Japa according to rule."

उपस्पृश्य द्विजो नित्यमन्नमद्यात्समाहितः ।
भुत्त्का चोपस्पृशेत्सम्यगन्द्रिः खानि च संस्पृशेत् ॥[72]

"Having washed, the twice-born should eat food always with a collected mind; having eaten, let him rinse well and sprinkle the sense-organs with water."

ज्ञानं तपोऽग्निराहारो मृन्मनो वार्युपाञ्जनम् ।
वायुः कर्मार्ककालौ च शुद्धेः कर्त्तृणिा देहिनाम् ॥[73]

"Wisdom, austerity, fire, food, earth, mind, water, plastering, wind, rites, the sun and time are the purifiers of bodies."

70 *Manusmriti,* vi—151.

71 *Ibid* ii—222,

72 *Ibid. ii*—53.

73 *Ibid,* v—105.

अन्द्रिर्गात्राणिा शुध्यन्ति मनः सत्येन शुध्यति ।
विद्यातपोभ्यां भूतात्मा वुद्धिर्ज्ञानेन शुध्यति ॥[74]

"The body is purified by water, the mind by truth, the soul by knowledge and austerity, the reason by wisdom."

नहि ज्ञानेन सद्दशं पवित्रमिह विद्यते ।[75]

"Verily there is no purifier in this world like wisdom."

अपि चेत्सुदुराचारो भजते मामनन्यभाक् ।
साधुरेव स मंतव्यः सम्यग्व्यवसितो हिसः ॥
क्षिप्रं भंवति धर्मात्मा शक्ष्वच्छान्तिं निगच्छति ।
कौंतेय प्रतिजानीहि न मे भक्तः प्रणाश्यति ॥[76]

"Even if the most sinful worship Me with undivided heart, he too must be accounted righteous, for he hath rightly resolved;

"Speedily he becometh dutiful and goeth to everlasting peace. Know thou, O Kaunteya, that my devotee perisheth never."

CHAPTER 4

THE FIVE DAILY SACRIFICES

We have seen that there exists a law of Yajna, of Sacrifice, and that man's glory is to voluntarily work with it. We have now to see how the Sanatana Dharma trained its followers to this end.

We may pass over, for the present, the numerous sacrifices of

74 *Manusmriti, v* –109.

75 *Bhagavad-Gita,* iv–38.

76 *Ibid*, ix, 30–31,

variuos kinds laid down in the sacred books, and concern ourselves only with the "Great sacrifices" to be offered every day. These are:—

The Sacrifice to Rishi or Vedas.

The Sacrifice to Devas.

The Sacrifice to Pitris.

The Sacrifice to Men.

The Sacrifice to Bhutas.

Each of these has an outer form and inner meaning, and the latter leads the sacrficer on to the full life of sacrifice. Let us try to understand both.

The outer sacrifice to the Rishis, or Vedas, is study and teaching. Every day a man should[77] study some sacred book, and thus gradually acquire the knowledge without which he cannot rightly understand himself, his position and his duties. And he should ever he ready to share this knowledge with those more ignorant than himself: hence Manu, in describing this sacrifice, calls it teaching. A boy should daily offer this sacrifice, reading and carefully thinking over some shlokas from the *Bhagavad-Gita,* the *Anugita, Hams a Gita* or other sacred work. The carefulness and closeness of the thought is more important than the amount read. The inner meaning is that all study should be a sacrifice, learning in order that we may teach.

The outer sacrifice to the Devas is the Homa, the recognition of all we owe to the kindly ministry and protection of this active Intelligences working in nature, and the repayment of it by giving for their service a share of our possessions. The inner meaning is the realisation of our relations with the super-physical worlds, and of the inter-dependence of the worlds. We must learn to be in harmony with nature, in accord with all that lives.

The outer sacrifice to the Pitris is the Tarpan or offering of water, to the older generations of our family, to our ancestors. The inner meaning is the recognition of the great debt we owe to

77 See *Manusmriti,* iii—70.

the past, to the generations who occupied the earth before us. and who toiled and laboured that they might hand it on, improved, and enriched, to us, their posterity. No man is truly human who does not recognise what he owes to the past, his debt to the ancestors.

The outer sacrifice to Men is hospitality: every day a true Aryan should feed some one poorer than himself. The inner meaning is the duty of serving and helping humanity, of feeding the hungry, clothing the naked, sheltering the homeless, comforting the sad. Those who are rich are the stewards of the poor.

The outer sacrifice to Bhutas, to creatures, is the putting of a little food on the ground, before beginning the meal, for the invisible lower entities around us, and the placing of the remains of the meal in a suitable place for vagrant men and animals. The inner meaning is the duty of caring for those who are beneath us in the human and in the lower kingdoms, the recognition of our debt to them for their services to us, and the practice of kindness and consideration towards them.

Thus the five great daily sacrifices teach man his relations, with all around him, with his superiors, his equals, and his inferiors. They establish the harmonious relations on which the happiness and prosperity o£ families and of nations depend. They turn the wheel of life in accord with the will of Ishvara, and so help on the evolution of the worlds. They teach each individual that he is not an isolated unit, but a part of a great whole, a cell in a vast body: and that his happiness and progress, therefore, can only be secure if they subserve the general happiness, and conduce to the general progress.

श्रध्यापनं ब्रह्मयज्ञः पितृयज्ञस्तु तर्पणाम् ।
होमो दैवो बलिर्भौतो नृयज्ञोऽतिथिपूजनम् ॥[78]

"Teaching is the Brahma-sacrifice, Tarpana is the Pitri-sacrifice, Homa (the offering into the fire) is the Deva-sacrifice, Bali (food) is

78 *Manusmriti* iii—70.

the Bhuta-sacrifice, hospitality to guests the. Manushya- sacrifice."

स्वाध्याये नित्ययुक्तः स्याहैव चैवेह कर्मणि ।
दैवे कर्मणियुक्तो हि विभर्तीदं चराचरम् ॥[79]

"Let a man ever engage in Veda-study, and in the rites of the Devas; engaged in the rites of the Devas he supporteth the movable and immovable kingdoms."

ऋषयः पितरो देवा भूतान्यतिथयस्तथा ।
श्राशासते कुटुम्बिभ्यस्तेभ्यः कार्यं विज्ञनता ॥
स्वाध्यायेनार्चयेतर्षीन् होमैर्देववान्यथाविधि ।
पितृञ्छ्राद्धेन नृनन्नैर्भूतानि बलिकर्मणा ॥[80]

"The Rishis, the Pitris, the Devas, the Bhutas, and guests expect (help) from the householders; hence he who knoweth should give unto them.

"Let him worship, according to the rule, the Rishis with Veda-study, the Devas with Homa, the Pitris with Shraddha, men with food, and the Bhutas with Bali.''

CHAPTER 5

WORSHIP

The performance of the five daily sacrifices by man as an inter-dependent part of a universe, does not, however, completely satisfy the longings of the truly religious man. He longs to come into conscious relations with the Lord of the Universe, with Ishvara, with

79 *Ibid,* iii—80, 81,

80 *Ibid*, iii—75.

the great Life of which his own is a part. This need of man finds its satisfaction in worship. When Vyasa, master of the final truth of Para-Brahma and ever working for the good of all beings, after he had written even the *Mahabharatam* and the *Brahma-satras* for the instruction of men, still found not peace of mind, Narada counselled him to sing the praise of Ishvara; and this he did in the *Vishnu-Bhagavata,* winning thereby the peace he did not gain before.[81]

Worship is the expression of love to the Supreme, of reverence towards Him, of aspiration to reach Him in conscious communion, of longing to be united with him, to feel the unity of the individual self with the supreme Self. It may take the form of praise of His Perfection, of prayer rooted in a sense of imperfection, of appeal to His Love, of recognition of His Power, of meditation on His Nature, of ntense longing for His Unveiling—and many another, according to the temperament and the stage of evolution of the worshipper. But whether in the peasant or in the philosopher, it is the expression or the longing after Brahman; the expression differs with the emotional and intellectual evolution, but the root-longing is the same.

The All, the Unconditioned, is never an Object of worship. Attributes are needed for worship, on which the mind can be fixed, by which the emotions can be stirred. The Saguna Brahman, Ishvara, is the Object of worship, whom all prayers and praises reach, to whom all contemplation is directed He may be adored as Shiva or Vishnu, as Mabadeva or Narayana, as Durga or Lakshmi, as Ganesha, Indra, Agni, Sarasvati, or as an Avatara—Kama, or Krishna, or Buddha; but under whatever name and form, it is Ishvara who is worshipped.

This explains a matter that often puzzles boys, why sometimes Shiva, sometimes Vishnu, is spoken of as the Supreme Being, why one Purana exalts One and another exalts Another All these are Forms; and Ishvara is One. The worshipper is worshipping Ishvara,

81 *Vishnv Bhagavata,* I, iv—v.

and is thinking of Ishvara, under the Form which he loves best. He is not worshipping the Form, hut the Lord in the Form —as a wife loves her husband, not the clothes he wears, though even those may be dear for the sake of the wearer. The worshipper worships the Love, the Beauty, the Power of Ishvara, as revealed in some one of His Divine Forms. We can only grasp a little, being small, but we grasp in our worship parts of the one Lord.

This is why the quarrels of different religions, and of different sects in the same religion, are so foolish and so ignorant. All are worshipping the same Ishvara, and the differences are only differences of names, due to differences in the worshippers, not in the Object of worship.

Puja is the general simple form of worship. A picture or image is used, mantras are recited, dowers are offered, water is poured out, and in these outer forms the inner love finds expression, and then rises beyond the forms to the Object thus served. The Form selected as representing the Object is sometimes the family Deva or Devi, and sometimes is the Ishtadeva, the Form chosen by the worshipper himself, or by his Guru for him.

Upasana is a term that includes many forms of worship, including meditation, and the daily Sandhya, which should be performed by all followers of the Sanatana Dharma. There are two forms of Sandhya, the Vaidika and the Tantrika, and a boy should perform the Sandhya according to his caste and family customs. He learns it from a properly qualified instructor, and should then practise it daily. Meditation, in its definite stages, belongs to manhood rather than to boyhood.

नैष्कर्म्यमप्युतभाववर्जितं न शौभते ज्ञानमलं निञ्जनम् ।
कुतः पुनः शक्ष्वदभद्रमीक्ष्वरे न चार्मितं कर्मयदप्यकारणम् ।।[82]

"Even the highest and most stainless knowledge, even perfect unselfishness in actions, shine not if uninspired by devotion to the

82 *Vishnu-Bhagarata*, I, v—12.

Imperishable. How then shall acts (bring peace) which (aim at fruit and) are not pure, or even those that are performed without desire, if they are not offered up to Ishvara?"

ये त्वक्षरमनिर्देश्यमव्यक्तं पर्युपासते ।
....
ते प्राप्नुवन्ति मामेव सर्वभूतहिते रताः ॥
क्लेशोऽधिकतरस्तेषामव्यक्तासक्तचेतसाम् ।
अव्यक्ता हि गतिर्दुःखं देहवद्भिरवाप्यते ॥
ये तु सर्वाणि कर्माणि मयि संन्यस्य मत्पराः ।
अनन्येनैवयोगेन मां ध्यायन्त उपासते ॥
तेषामहं समुद्धर्ता मृत्युसंसारसागरात् ।
भवामि न चिरात्पार्थ ! मय्यावेशितचेतसाम् ॥[83]

"They who worship the Indestructible, the Ineffable, the Unmanifested... ever working for the welfare of all creatures, these all come to me.

"The difficulty of those whose minds are set on the Unmanifested is greater; for the path of the Unmanifested is hard for the embodied to reach.

Those verily who, renouncing all actions in Me and Intent on Me, worship, meditating on Me with whole-hearted Yoga.

"Those I speedily lift up from the ocean of death and existence, O Partha, their minds being fixed on me."

ईश्वरः सर्वभूतानां हृद्देशेऽर्जुन ! तिष्ठति ।
भ्रामयन्सर्वभूतानियन्त्रारूढानि मायसा ॥
तमेव शरणां सर्वभावेन भारत ।
तत्प्रसादात्परां शान्ति स्थान प्राप्स्यसि शाक्ष्वतम् ॥[84]

83 *Bhagavad-Gita,,* xii, 3-7

84 *Ibid,* xviii, 61 – 62

The Lord dwelleth in the hearts of all beings, O Arjuna, causing all beings to revolve by His illusive power, as though mounted on a wheel.

"Flee unto Him for shelter with all thy being, O Bharata; by His grace thou shalt obtain susuprem peace and the everlasting dwelling place."

येयथा मां प्रपद्यन्ते तांस्तथैव भजाभ्यहम् ।
मम वर्त्मानुवर्तन्ते मनुष्याः पार्थ सर्वशः ॥[85]

"However men approach Me, even so do I welcome them, for the path men take from every side is mine, O Partha."

योयोयांयां तनुं भक्तः श्रद्धयार्चितुमिच्छति ।
तस्य तस्याचलां श्रद्धां तामेव विदधाम्यहम् ॥[86]

"Any devotee who seeketh to worship with faith any such aspect, I verily bestow the unswerving faith of that man."

CHAPTER 6

THE FOUR ASHRAMAS

Nations have characteristics, just as have individuals, and among the characteristics of the Hindu nation in old days were order and balance The Sanatana Dharma stamped these characteristics on the people, and thus shaped a very dignified type of man, evenly developed and well balanced. So much are these the characteristics

85 *Bhagavad-Gita,* iv...II.
86 *Ibid,* vii—21

of the true follower of the Sanatana Dharma, that Shri Krishna said: "Equilibrium is called Yoga."[87]

The large view of life taken in the Vedas is the root of these characteristics. All things exist for the sake of the Atma, the Self, and by his will. They exist merely to give him the experiences he desires to pass through. He wills to unfold his powers in the lower worlds, and to become the self-conscious Ruler of the outer realms of denser matter, as he is ever the Inner Ruler, Immortal. He is not in haste, being Eternal, and knows it best to take each experience in order, and thus to unfold symmetrically and harmoniously. This order is imposed by ishvara, the Supreme Self, on the lower kingdoms of our world; the seed, the root, the stem, the leaves, the flower, the fruit succeed each other in due order, and each has its place and its beauty in its season; so also He imposes the stages of human life—infancy, childhood, youth, maturity, old age; this sequence man can not escape from nor change; but the unfolding Jivatma in man, clouded by the matter he has not yet mastered, pushes irregularly in various directions, led by Manah dominated by Kama, grasping at the things of one stage while yet in another, and so hindering his due evolution in each. The child would be a youth, the youth a man; the old man grasps backward at the joys of youth; thus life is robbed of its serenity and thereby of half its usefulness.

In order to counteract this mistaken eagerness and lack of balanced order, the great Rishis marked out for the eldest-born family of the Aryan race the definite stages in the life of the individual from birth to death, and the definite stages in the life of the Jivatma in his long evolution through myriads of births and deaths. In each case these stages are four; in the life between one birth and one death they are called Ashramas, resting-places dwellings: in the life passing through countless, births and deaths they are called Varnas, colours, or castes.

---

87 *Bhagavad-Gita,* ii—48.

We are concerned here with the Ashramas. As said, these stages are four: Brahmacharya, the stage of studentship; Garhasthya, the stage of house- holdership; Vanaprastha, the stage of forest-dwelling, *i.e.,* seclusion; Sannyasa, the stage of total renunciation, *i. e.,* asceticism.[88]

In none of these stages must the man grasp at the special duties of the other three; the student must not be a householder, a recluse, or an ascetic; the householder must not he a celibate, a recluse, or an ascetic; the recluse must not seek again the joys of the household; nor must the ascetic long after the quiet attachments of the recluse. Each stage has its own duties and its own pleasures. Discharged and enjoyed each in its own stage, they lead to the orderly unfolding of the Jivatma; when the Ashramas are disregarded, his evolution is delayed.

Now in modern days the Ashramas cannot be exactly lived according to the details of the ancient rules, the conditions having changed so much; but if we get a clear idea of the fundamental duties of each, we shall still he able to shape the life to an orderly course of development.

The life of the student begins with the Upanayana ceremony, his "second birth," and from that time forward certain virtues must be striven for by the boy. He must be hardy and simple in his habits; these virtues make his body strong and healthy; he acquires them by rising early, bathing, eating moderately of plain food, taking plenty of exercise, not allowing himself to lounge luxuriously and idly. Contrast a boy who lives in this way with one who lies late in bed, who over-eats himself on sweetmeats and rich dishes, who takes little exercise, and spends much of his time lying on soft pillows. The one is alert, strong, hard-muscled, vigorous, active, and will be a strong healthy man: the other is heavy, flabby, fat, lazy or too thin and weak, and will soon be diseased and suffering.

---

88 See *Manusmriti,* vi–87.

The student must also strive for the virtues of industry, obedience, humility and serviceableness; youth is the preparation-time of life, and industrious study to acquire knowledge is absolutely necessary for useful manhood; obedience is using the experience of his elders to guide his conduct, and saves him many a trouble in early life, and only he who knows how to obey is lit to rule here-after; humility lifts him quickly, as all are willing to share what they have with the humble; and serviceableness in the narrow circle of the family and the school builds up the nature that will serve humanity.

The student must be chaste in thought and act, a celibate in mind and body. He must guard his thoughts, for the boy who does not think impurity will not act imparity. He should not think of sex, nor yield to day-dreaming. Only the pure in thought and in body can pass unstained into happy household life. The very name of the student is the Brahmachari, which has come now to mean almost exclusively the celibate. Premature age, weakness, disease, race-decay, spring from student-marriage, against the ancient law.

The household stage is entered at marriage, when the, youth has completed his school and college career, and is ready to take up the duties and responsibilities of household life. Of ail the Ashramas this is the most important, for it sup ports all the others.* The welfare alike of the family and of the nation depends on the house-holder, and their happiness and prosperity are in his hands. A good husband, a good lather, a good master, a good citizen, is the noblest of men The home is the school of unselfishness, compassion, tenderness, temperance, purity, helpfulness, prudence, industry. right judgment, charity. The qualities that make the good householder, when shown to his own circle in house and State, are the qualities that make the Sage and the Saint when shown to all. The degradation of the ideal of the householder has made modern life petty and sordid, and the half entrance into it. and the confusion of its duties with those of the student, caused by the modern evil of student-marriage has deprived the entry into it of its ancient solemnity and dignity. The plucking and eating of unripe fruit deprives the eater of its sweetness.

Certain well-born but thoughtless Brahmana youths abandoning their homes before due time, went into the forests to lead a life of asceticism. Indra pitied them, and, assuming the form of a golden bird, taught them: "Follow the household life! *It* is the field for the cultivation of virtues. It is sacred. Worship of the Devas, study, repayment of the debt to the pitris by the rearing of a family and helping on new lives as we have beer, reared and helped—these are the austerest of penances. Bear the heavy burthen of the duties of the household! They that run away from their work fall into sin. To eat the remnant of the food left after helping the needy is to eat the true remnant of sacrifice.[89]

When the householder sees his sons able to bear the full burden of his duties, when the signs of age appear, and his children's children are round him, the time has come for him and his wife to surrender the headship of the home, and to retire from active life and worldly labour. A quiet and somewhat secluded life, given to study, to self-sacrifice for the good of others, to the counselling of the younger, such should be the third Ashrama in our modern days.

Finally in old age a man may rightly enter the fourth Ashrama, that of the ascetic, passing his last days in meditation and worship, till he enters willingly the life beyond death, to reap the fruits of a well spent earthly life, hereafter to return for further evolution.

ब्रह्मचारी गृहस्थश्च वानप्रस्थीयतिंस्तथा ।
एते गृहस्थप्रभवाश्यत्वारः पृथगाश्रमाः ॥[90]

"The student, the householder, the forest-dweller, the ascetic—these, the four separate orders, spring from the householder."

89 See *Mantwnriti,* iii, 77, and 89—9O.

90 *Mantwnriti,* vi—37.

वेदानधीत्य वेदौ वा वेदं वापियथाक्रमस् ।
अविप्लुतब्रह्मचर्यो गृहस्थाश्रममावसेत् ॥
गृहस्थस्तुयदा पश्येद्वलीपलितमात्मनः ।
अपत्यस्य तथापत्यं तदारणयं समाश्रयेत् ॥
वनेषु तु विहृत्यैवं तृतीयं भागमायुषः ।
चतुर्थमायुषो भागं त्यक्त्वा संगान् परिव्रजेत् ॥[91]

"Having studied the Vedas, or two Vedas, or even one Veda, in due order, without violating celibacy, let him enter the household-order.

"When the householder sees wrinkles (on his skin), whiteness (in his hair), and the progeny of his progeny, then let him retire to the forest.

"Having passed the third portion of his life in the forest, let him abandon all attachments and wander (as an ascetic) the fourth portion of his life."

अनधीत्य द्विजो वेदाननुत्पाद्य तथा प्रजाम् ।
अनिष्ट्वा चैवयशैश्च मोक्षमिच्छन् व्रजत्यधः ॥[92]

"A twice-born man who seeketh Moksha without having studied the Vedas, without having produced offspring, and without having offered sacrifices, goeth downwards."

अनारोग्यमनायुष्यमस्वर्ग्यं चातिभोजनम् ।
अपुण्यं लोकविद्विष्टं तस्मात्तत्परिवर्जयेत् ॥[93]

''Over-eating is against health, long life, (the attainment of)

91 Idid. iii—2 and vi, 2—33.

92 Manusmriti, vi—37.

93 ibid, ii—57.

heaven and merit, and is disapproved by the world; therefore let it be avoided"

नोदितो गुरुणा नित्यमप्रणोदित एव वा ।
कुर्यादध्ययनेयत्नमाचार्यस्य हितेषु च ।
....
वर्जयेन्मधु मांसं च गंधं माल्यं रसान्स्त्रियः ।
शुक्तानि चेद्य सर्वाणि प्राणिनां चैव हिंसनम् ॥
कामं क्रोधं च लोभं च नर्तनं गीतवादनम् ।
द्यूतं च जनवादं च परिवादं तथानृतम् ॥
....
एकः शयीत सर्वत्र न रेतः स्कंदयेत् क्वचित् ।
कामाद्धि स्कंदयन् च परिवादं तथानृतम्ः ॥[94]

"Directed or not directed by his teacher, let the student ever engage in study, and in doing services to his preceptor."

"Let the student refrain from wine, meat, perfumes, garlands, tasty and savoury dishes, women, acids, and injury to sentient creatures"

"From lust, anger and greed, dancing, singing, and playing on musical instruments, from diceplaying, gossip, slander and from untruth"

"Let the student always sleep alone, and let him not waste his seed; he, who from lust wasteth his seed, destroyeth his vow."

यथा वायुं समाश्रित्य सर्वे जीवन्ति जन्तवः ।
तथा गृहस्थमाश्रित्य वर्तन्त इतराश्रमाः ॥
सर्वेषामपि चैतेषां वेदश्रुतिविधानतः ।
गृहस्थ उच्यते श्रेष्ठः स त्रीनेतान् बिभर्तिहि ॥

94 *Manusmriti.* ii, 191, 177—18O.

तथा नदीनदाः सर्वे समुद्रेयान्ति संस्थितिम् ।
तथैवाश्रमिणाः सर्वे गृहस्थेयान्ति संस्थितिम् ।।[95]

"As all creatures live supported by the air, so the other orders exist supported by the house-holder.

"Of all these (Ashramas), by the declaration of the Veda-scripture, the householder is the highest; he verily supporteth the other three.

As all streams and rivers flow to rest in the ocean, so all the Ashramas flow to rest in the householder."

अनाश्रितः कर्मफलं कार्यं कर्म करोतियः ।
सत्संन्यासी सयोगी च न निरग्निर्न चाक्रियः ।।[96]

"He that performeth such action as in duty, independently of the fruit of action, he is a Sannyasi, he is a Yogi, not he that is without fire and without rites.

CHAPTER 7

THE FOUR CASTES

In the long pilgrimage of the Jivatma through myriads of births, already referred to, there are four distinctly marked stages, called of old Vareas, or colours, and recognised in the social polity laid down by Manu as distinct social classes, or castes.

These stages are universal, all Jivatmas passing through them; the peculiarity of the Sanatana Pharma is that it has made them the framework of its social polity. In the early days the outer

95 Ibid, iii, 77, 89—90

96 Bagavad-Gita, vi—1.

caste coincided with the stages: Jivatmas at each stage were born into bodies belonging to that stage, and the whole of society was therefore contented and progressive. But in these later days, as Arjuna truly foresaw in his distress on Kurukshetra. varnasankara, caste-confusion, has come on Aryavarta and her whole peninsula. Jivatmas at each stage are. being born into bodies of other stages, and hence, as surely as content and progress arose out of the harmony of elder days, do disorder and stagnation arise out of the disharmony of the present. How a better state of things may be brought about is a question for men to discuss and resolve, not for inexperienced boys. What we need here is to understand the meaning of caste.

We have said there are four stages.

The first is that which includes the infancy, childhood and youth of the Jivatma; he is unfolding youthful virtues, developing obedience, serviceableness, patience; he has few responsibilities; his duties may be summed up in the word, Service. Where there is no caste-confusion, such young Jivatmas are born only into the lower social stratum; they are labourers, artisans, servants, manual workers of every kind. In the social polity of the Santana Dharma, such Jivatmas were born into the caste of Shudras. In these days of caste-confusion, such young Jivatmas, whether born into the Shudra caste in India, or into the corresponding class elsewhere, are happy, contented and useful; but where, as often happens now-a-days, they are born into higher castes, or classes, they do much harm to their surroundings by their incapacity to discharge higher duties, and to bear the weight of higher responsibilities. So also difficulties arise when older Jivatmas are born into the lower bodies, and fret against their environment, are discontented and rebellious. Of course a really advanced Jivatma is content in any body, but the mediocre Jivatmas quite naturally and inevitably fight against uncongenial surroundings, and their restlessness is used by Ishvara to help on evolution and to bring about necessary changes.

The second stage covers the first half of the Jivatma's manhood, when he is fit to gain wealth, to enjoy it and use it, to organise labour and direct it, to undertake great responsibilities, and administer well accumulated possessions. This includes the commercial class, the great traders, and the organisers of industry, the capitalists, bankers, the managers of large industrial concerns. In the social polity of the Sanatana Pharma, such Jivatmas were born into the caste of Vaishyas, and were trained in it gradually to see as aim the common good and the general prosperity, instead of mere personal aggrandisement.

The third stage makes the second half of the Jivatma's manhood, when his responsibilities and powers widen out to include the nation, and he is called to legislate, to rule, to work unselfishly for the State, and to use his power to protect and to regulate, not to aggrandise himself. This includes kings, judges, legislators, warriors, all who rule and keep order in the State. In the social polity of the Sanatana Pharma, such mature Jivatmas were born into the Kshattriya caste, and bore the burden of kingship and of fighting for the national defence.

The fourth stage embraces the serene age of the Jivatma, when earthly things have lost their charm, and he becomes the counsellor and friend and helper of all his youngers. This includes the priests, the counsellors, the teachers of every kind —authors, scientists, poets, philosophers. In the social polity of the Sanatana Dharma, such Jivatmas were born into the caste of Brahmanas, the advanced and unselfish ones who gave much and needed little. Caste-confusion in India has struck this caste most hardly, as the degradation of the higher is always worse than that of the lower. The Shudra Jivatma in the Brahmana body is the greatest danger to the Sanatana Pharma.

Much of the evil has grown from men of each caste grasping at the work of the other castes, and from each thinking more of the rights his caste gives him than of the duties it imposes. The Brahmana and the Kshattriya have claimed their privileges ardently, and have shrunk from the heavy burdens belonging to their castes. Naturally this attitude has provoked opposition, and antagonisms have replaced mutual service and good-will. Hence caste has become a source of social bitterness, instead of a framework maintaining all in happy order.

At least this much every boy can do towards bringing about a happier state of things: he can diligently practise the virtues characteristic of his caste, and avoid pride, vanity, and grasping at privileges. Let the Shudra be remarkable for his industry, fidelity and serviceableness; let the Vaishya be remarkable for his diligence, discretion and charity; let the Kshattriya be remarkable for his courage, generosity and vigour; let the Brahmana be remarkable for his patience, purity, learning, truthfulness and self-sacrifice. And it may be that, if the castes thus practise their several Dharmas, caste-confusion may gradually pass away.

ब्राह्मणोऽस्य मुखमासीद्वाहू राजन्यः कृतः ।
ऊरू तदस्ययद्वैश्यः पद्भयां शूद्रो अजायत ।।[97]

"The Brahmana was His mouth; the Rajanya was made His two arms; His two thighs the Vaishya; the Shudra was born from His two feet."

सर्वस्यास्य तुं सर्गस्य गुप्त्सर्थे स महाद्युतिः ।
मुखवाहूरुपज्जानां पृथकर्मारायकल्पयत् ।।
अध्यापनमध्ययनंयजनंयाजनं तथा ।
दानं प्रतिग्रहं चैव ब्राह्मणानामकल्पयत् ।।
प्रजानां रक्षणं दानमिज्याध्ययनमेव च ।
विषयेष्वप्रसक्तिं च क्षत्रियस्य समादिशत् ।।
पशूनां रक्षणां दानमिज्याध्ययनमेव ।

97 Ragveda, X, xo—12.

वणिक्पथं कुसदिं च वैश्यस्य कृषिमेव च ॥
एकमेवं तु शूद्रस्य प्रभुः कर्म समादिशत् ।[98]
एतेषामेव वर्णानां शुश्रूषामनसूयया ॥

''He, the Resplendent, for the sake of protecting all this creation, assigned separate karmas to those born of His mouth, arms, thighs and feet.

"Teaching and studying the Veda, sacrificing and also guiding others in offering sacrifices, gifts and receiving of gifts, these He assigned to the Brahmanas.

"The protection of the people, gifts, sacrificing, and study of the Vedas, non-attachment amid the objects of the senses, these He prescribed to the Kshattriyas.

"The protection of cattle, gifts, sacrificing, and study of the Vedas, commerce, banking, and agriculture, to the Vaishyas.

"The Lord commanded one karma only for the Shudras, to serve ungrudgingly these other castes."

यस्ययल्लक्षणं प्रोक्तं पुंसो वर्णाभिव्यंञ्जकम् ।
यदन्यत्रापि द्दश्येतः तत् तेनैव विनिर्दिशेत् ॥

"What is said as to the marks (of conduct) indicative of a man's caste, if those marks are found in another, let him he designated by the caste of his marks (and not of his birth)."

नयोनिर्नापि संस्कारो न श्रुतं न च सन्ततिः ।
कारणानि द्विजत्वस्य वृत्तमेव तु कारणम् ॥

"Not birth, nor Samskaras, nor study of the Vedas, nor ancestry, are the causes of being Twice-born. Conduct alone is verily the cause thereof."

98 *Manusmriti,* 87—91.

सत्यं दानं क्षमा शीलमानृशंस्यं तपोघृणा ।
दृश्यतेयत्रं नागेन्द्र स ब्राह्मणा इति स्मृतः ॥
शूद्रे तुयद्भवेल्लक्ष्मं द्विजे तत्रं न विद्यते ।
नैव शूद्रोभवेच्छूद्रो ब्राह्मणो न च ब्राह्मणः ।
यत्रैतल्लक्ष्यते सर्वं वृत्तं स ब्राह्मणः स्मृतः ।
यत्र नैतद्भवेत् सर्वं तं शूद्रमिति निर्दिशेत् ॥

"Truth, charity, forgiveness, good conduct, gentleness, austerity, and mercy, where these are seen, O king of serpents, he is called a Brahmana.

"If these marks exist in a Shudra, and not in one twice-born, the Shudra, is not a Shudra, nor the Brahmana a Brhahmana.

"Where this conduct is shown, O serpent, he is called a Brahmana; where this is not, O serpent, he should be regarded as a Shudra."

श्राचारहीनं न पुनन्ति वेदायद्यप्यधीताः सह षड्भिरङ्गैः ।
छन्दांस्येनं मृत्युकाले त्यजन्ति नीडं शकुन्ता इव जातपक्षाः ॥
आचारहीनस्य तु ब्राह्मणस्य वेदा प्रडङ्गैस्त्वखिलाः सयशाः ।
कां प्रीतिमुत्पादपितुं समर्था श्रन्धस्य दारा इव दर्शनीयाः ॥[99]

"The Vedas help not the man that hath not righteous ways, even though they be studied to-gether with all the angas. The Chhandas abandon him at the supreme moment of death, even as full- fledged birds their nest.

"To the Brahmana that is void of righteous ways, the Vedas, even in their entirety, and With all angas and all sacrifices too, can bring no more joy than a wife, lovely to see, can bring unto a blind husband."

99 vas*ishtha-Smriti*, vi, 3—4.

PART III

ETHICAL TEACHINGS

CHAPTER 1

ETHICAL SCIENCE, WHAT IT IS

Science is a definitely arranged body of knowledge, of facts related to each other. A collection of facts does not make a science; the facts must be. systematically arranged in their relations to each other, and the principles underlying these relations must be known, before the collection can be called a science. Ethical means that which relates to conduct, to the way in which rational beings should behave towards each other as well as towards other creatures. When, therefore, we speak of Ethical Science, we do not mean a list of virtues and vices, but we mean a definite and systematically arranged series of facts of conduct in their proper relations to each other and of the underlying principles of these relations.

Another word for Ethics is morality, right conduct, and in order to know what is right we have to understand something about man and his surroundings.

The object of morality is to secure the welfare of all beings, and this is done by showing men, through the science of Conduct, how to live in harmony with each other and with their surroundings. Ishvara is Love, and wills the happiness of His universe, is gradually bringing about universal happiness. This does not mean that a right thing always is pleasant, and a wrong thing always unpleasant, for the time; but it means that the conduct which leads to lasting happiness, to the bliss of union with Ishvara, to Moksha in the end, is good. "As the wheels of the cart follow the ox, so misery follows sin," and so also happiness follows righteousness.

The fruit of wrong-doing may be sweet to the taste in the eating, but it is poison, and brings about bitter pain afterwards, and sometimes long-continued disease. The boy who does wrong because it gives him a short pleasure is like the ignorant child who plucks and eats the sweet gaily coloured poison-berries that make him in the evening writhe in pain. It is the duty of the teacher of morality to mark every sin as "Poison."

श्राचारलक्षणो धर्मः संतस्त्वाचारलक्षणः ।
श्रागमानां हि सर्वेषामाचारः श्रेष्ठ उच्यते ॥
श्राचारप्रभवो धर्मो धर्मादायुर्विवर्धते ।
श्राचाराल्लभते ह्यायुराचाराल्लभते श्रियम् ॥
श्राचारात्कीर्त्तिमाप्नोति पुरुषः प्रेत्य चेह च ॥[100]

"The mark of Dharma is Achara (good conduct). Achara is the mark of the good. Higher than all teachings is Achara. From Achara is Pharma born, and Pharma enhances life. By Achara man attains life. By Achara he attains fame, here and hereafter.

श्राचारः परमो धर्मः श्रुत्युक्तः स्मार्त एव च ।
तस्मादस्मिन् सदायुक्तो नित्यं स्यादात्मवांन् द्विजः ॥
एवमाचारतो हष्ट्रा धर्मस्य मुनयो गतिम् ।
सर्वस्य तपसो मूलमाचारं जगृहुः परम् ॥

"Achara is the highest Dharma, declared by the Shruti and the Smriti. Therefore let the Twice-born that knoweth the Self ever diligently engage therein.

"Thus beholding the path of Pharma issue from Achara, the sages embraced Achara as the root of all Tapas.

---

100 *Makabkarata,* AnushiKaiia Parva, civ.

प्रभवार्थाय भूतानां धर्मप्रवचनं कृतम् ।
यः स्यात्प्रभवसंयुक्तः स धर्म इति निश्चयः ॥
धारणाद्धर्ममित्याहुर्धर्मेण विधृताः प्रजाः ।
यः स्याद्धारणसंयुक्तः स धर्म इति निश्चयः ॥
श्रहिंसार्थाय भूतानां धर्मप्रवचनं कृतम् ।
यः स्यादहिंसयायुक्तः स धर्म इति निश्चयः ॥
सर्वेषांयः सुहृन्नित्यं सर्वेषां च हिते रतः ।
कर्मणा मनसा वाचा स धर्मं वेद जाजले ॥

"For the well-being of all beings was pharma declared. That only which bringeth such well-being is Dharma. This is sure.

"Because it supporteth and holdeth together it is called Dharma. By Dharma are the peOple upheld. That which upholdeth is alone Dharma. This is sure.

"For the making harmless of beings was Dharma declared. That which secureth preservation of beings is pharma. This is sure.

"He who is the friend of all beings; he who is intent on the welfare of all with act and thought and speech—he only knoweth Pharma, O Jajali."

न कुर्यात्कर्हिचित्संगं तमत्तीव्रं तितीरिषुः ।
धर्मार्थकाममोक्षाणांयदत्यन्तविद्यातकम् ॥
तत्रापि मोक्ष एवार्थ आत्यन्तिकतयेष्यते ।
त्रैवर्ग्योऽर्थोयतो नित्य कृतान्तभयसंयुतः ॥[101]

"He who wishes to cross beyond this intense darkness, let him not attach himself too much to anything, for (such attachment) is the great frustrator of Pharma (religion, etc.), Artha (wealth), Kama (pleasure) and Moksha (emancipation).

101 *Vishnu Bhagavata,* IV, xxii, 34—35.

"Of these (four) too, Moksha is the truly ultimate end, for the other three are ever haunted by the fear of Death, the Ender."

धर्मं चार्थं च कामं चयथावद्वदतां वर ।
विभज्य काले कालज्ञः सर्वान् सेवेत पण्डितः ॥
मोक्षो वा मरणं श्रेय एषां राजन्सुखार्थिनाम् ।[102]

"The wise man, O best of speakers, that knoweth the proper times, serveth Dharma, Artha and Kama, all three evenly, dividing his time between them (on the Pravritti Marga, the path of outgoing).

"But, O King, all beings desire happiness, and Moksha (belonging to the Nivrtti Marga, the path of return) is the highest good for them."

CHAPTER 2

THE FOUNDATION OF ETHICS AS GIVEN BY RELIGION

We have already seen that the first proclamation of Religion is "The Self is One." There are indeed many selves in appearance, but they are all portions or reflections of the One. Their separateness is temporary, their unity is eternal. Many pots may be dipped into a tank, but the water that fills each is the same water. Many upadhis are dipped into the ocean of existence, but the life that fills each is the same life. This primary truth of religion is the foundation of Ethics.

We must, then, in our Ethical Science recognise the unity of the Self. But this is not enough, for in unity there is neither "I"

102 *Mahabharatam*. Vana Parva, xxxiii, 41—42.

nor "You," and we have seen that our science deals with relations between "I" and "You." So we must also recognise the "diversity of the Not-Self;" that means that there are many upadhis of mutter, and in each separate upadhi there is a part, or reflection, of the One Self. There are innumerable bodies, innumerable minds, and these bodies and minds come into relations with each other. There-run never be right relations until each separate mind and body act to other minds and bodies on the principle that they are at root one, that what helps all is the only thing that really helps each, and that what injures one really injures all. In hurting another we are really hurting ourselves. If a hand cut the foot belonging to its own body, the blood would flow from the foot, not from the hand; hut presently the hand would grow weak, for the blood circulates in the whole body and there is only one supply for all parts of the body. So also with men; and if one man wounds another, the wounder suffers as much as the wounded, only the suffering takes longer in making itself felt.

This, then, is the foundation of right conduct, as seen by the Reason. Boys have at first to take moral precepts on the authority of great Sages and Saints, as taught in the Shastras, because they have not the power nor the time to think them out for themselves. But they can, in their manhood, verify these precepts, given in the Sanatana Dharma, by applying their Reason to them.

The One Self is in all beings; every Jivatma is a portion, or reflection, of the One Self. Let this principle sink deeply into every heart, and let each remember that he who injures another injures himself Sayeth Shri Krishna: "I am the Self, O Gudakesha, seated in the heart of all beings; I am the beginning, the middle, and also the end of beings.''[103]

एको देवः सर्वतभूेष गूढः
सर्वव्यापी सर्वभूतान्तरात्मा।

103 *Bhagavad-Gita x—20.*

कर्माध्यक्षः सर्वभूताधिवासः
साक्षी चेता केवलो निर्गुराश्र ।।[104]

"One God hideth in all beings. He pervadeth all. He is the inmost Self of all beings. He superviseth all actions. He is the resting-place of all beings. He is the Witness, the Consciousness, the One above limitations and qualities."

एकस्तथा सर्वभूतान्तरात्मारूपंरूपं प्रतिरूपो वभूव।[105]

"This one universal Inner Self of all beings becometh one separate individual self for each form."

यस्तु सर्वाणि भूतान्यात्मन्येवानुपश्यति।
सर्वभूतेषु चात्मानं ततो न विजुगुप्सते।।
यस्मिन् सर्वाणि भूतान्यात्मैवाभूद्विजानतः।
तत्र को मोहः कः शोक एकत्वपनुपश्यतः।।[106]

"He who seeth all beings in the Self, and the Self in all beings, he shrinketh no more (from any, in dislike)."

"He in whose consciousness, full of perfected knowledge, all beings have become the Self—in him, thus beholding the unity, there is no more any delusion nor any sorrow."

सर्वभूतस्थमात्मांन सर्वभूतानि चात्मनि।
ईक्षतेयोगयुत्त्वात्मा सर्वत्र समदर्शनः।।[107]

---

104 *Shretashvataropnishal,* vii—2.
105 *Kathopanishat*, v—10.
106 *Ishopanishat*, 6—7.
107 *Bhagavad-Gita*, vi—29.

"The self, harmonised by yoga, seeth the Self abiding in all beings, all beings, in the Self; every-where he seeth the same."

CHAPTER 3

RIGHT AND WRONG

These two words, Right and Wrong, are in the mouth of everybody, but it is not everybody who can tell us exactly what he means by right and wrong. Let us try to understand.

We have seen that we have specially to do with three worlds, the Triloki, and we know that the Triloki is created by Brahma, preserved by Vishnu, and dissolved by Shiva. Let us think of a new Triloki. It is a going forth; many forms appear, and grow and develop; they become more and more different; they involve into separate individuals; they grow by the experiences they meet; they develop their bodies and minds by taking all they can from outside and working it up into themselves. This is called the Pravritti Marga, the path of going forth, on which the Jivatma is building himself up into a separate individual, by taking all he can from outside, and making a strong intellect, a powerful "I." When this is complete, the Jivatma has to learn that he himself is only a part or reflection of a much greater "I," the Ishvara, and that all his powers can only bring happiness if used as a part of that greater "I.' Then he begins to see the Unity under the diversity, and turns away from his little separate self to realise the One Self; he tries to give to all that are weaker than he is, to share with himself in other bodies. and minds what he has accumulated in his own. This is called the Nivritti Marga, the path of return, on which the Jivatma is seeking to realise himself as one with all by sharing all he has with all who need.

These two paths make up what is called evolution, and along this road of evolution the Will of Ishvara, in His aspect of Vishnu, is guiding His universe. To work with this Will is Right; to work against it is Wrong.

Now the world, as a whole, is at the turning point where the Pravritti Marga changes to the Nivritti Marga. Most people are still on the Pravritti Marga, but their way onwards, their higher evolution, lies along the Nivritti Marga. Hence right conduct consists of the desires, thoughts and actions that help oneself and others to tread the Nivritti Marga, the path that leads to Union. We must aim at decreasing separateness, at increasing unity; all that lessons separateness, and leads towards unity is Eight; all that in-creases separateness and leads away from unity is Wrong. But for animals, savages, and backward, undeveloped Jivatmas, whose individuality is still very weak, separateness has still to be aimed at, and what is right or wrong for the more advanced is not yet right or wrong for them. This is what is meant by saying that morality is relative. It is related to our position in evolution, to the path we are on.

"Subtle is morality," Bhishma said to Yudhishthira. "I instruct thee not by the letter of the Veda alone, but by the Veda as interpreted by wisdom and experience. None may accomplish his course through the world aright with the help of a morality that is one-sided. The text of the Scripture should be applied with careful exercise of judgment, otherwise it faileth grievously. Ushans spake this truth in time of old, that Scriptures are no Scriptures if they cannot stand the test of reason. The presence of a knowledge that is full of doubts is no better than its absence. A morality that is based on words, without regard to special circumstances leads to error. In a time of long-continued famine, the Rishi Vishvamitra took forbidden meat from a chandala, and compelled the Devas to take their customary share from that same meat offered in sacrifice, and thus to justify his act. Forgiveness befits the Sannyasi; it does not always befit the King. The King may forgive injuries to himself. He may not overlook the slightest wrong done to the meanest of his subjects, if he wish himself and his country well. The sin that attaches to the killing of a person that should not be killed is equal to the sin of not slaying one that deserves to he slain. The King should ever exact with firmness, yea, severity, from all his subjects their respective duties. If he does not do this, then will they prowl about unchecked, like wolves, murdering the weaker and devouring each other. It has been sung of old: 'She alone is a wife that speaketh pleasantly. He alone is a son that maketh his sire happy. He alone is a friend who may be safely trusted. That, verily, is the motherland wherein living is earned.' He alone is a King who ruleth strictly without oppression, in whose territories the righteous have no fear, who cherisheth the poor and punisheth the wicked."

The Ashramas and the Varnas were given in order to shew people what kind of virtues they should aim at, in the particular place and time in which they find themselves, and thus to help on their orderly evolution. As all men have not the power nor the time to find out for themselves the Will of Ishvara, the Shastras have been given to tell us of that Will, and so to help us in distinguishing between Right and Wrong. But some general rules have also been laid down in the sacred books, by Vyasa and by others, for application in cases in which the details are not clear or specific, and therefore the special rules, given in the Shastras, not easy or necessary to apply. Such are:

"To give joy to another is righteousness; to give pain is sin."

"Let not any man do unto another any act that he wisheth not done to himself by others, knowing it to be painful to himself. And let him also purpose for another all that he wisheth for himself."

"Let not any one do an act that injureth another, nor any that he feeleth shame to do."

"Let him not do to another what is not good for himself."

सुखाभ्युदयिकं चैव नैश्रेयसिकमेव च।
प्रवृत्तं च निवृत्तं च द्विविधं कर्म वैदिकम्॥
इह चामुत्र वा काम्यं प्रवृत्तं कर्म कीर्त्यते।
निष्कामं ज्ञानपूर्वं तु निवृत्तमुपदिश्यते॥
प्रवृत्तं कर्म संसेव्य देवानमेति साभ्सताम्।
निवृत्तं सेवमानस्तु भूतान्यत्येति पंच वे॥[108]

"Of two kinds is the karma mentioned in the Vedas, Pravritta and Nivritta, leading to joys or leading to that (happiness) than which there is no higher.

"Karma done under personal desire (for gain), here or hereafter, is Pravritta Karma; done without such desire, under guidance of perfected knowledge (of right and duty) is Nivritta.

"Doing Pravritta Karma man evolves into the condition of Devas. Performing Nivritta he rises to beyond the five Bhutas."

अन्ये कृतयुगे धर्मास्त्रेतायां द्वापरे परे।
अन्ये कलियुगे नृणांयुगाह्रासनुरूपतः॥[109]

"Different are the dharmas in Krita-yuga; different in Treta and Dvapara; different again are the dharmas of men in Kali-Yuga—changing according to the changes of the cycles."

यतः प्रवृत्तिर्भूतानांयेन सर्वमिंद ततम्।
स्वकर्मणा तमभ्यर्च सिद्धिं विन्दति मानवः॥
श्रेयान् स्वधर्मो विगुणः परधर्मात्स्त्रनुष्ठितात्।
स्वभावनियंत कर्म कुर्वन्नाप्नोति किल्विषम्॥
ईश्वरः सर्वभूतानां हृद्देशे जुंन तिष्ठति।

108 *Manusmriti,* xxi—88, 89, 90.

109 Mahabharatam, Shanti Parva, ccxxxi—27.

भ्रामयन्सर्वभूतानियन्त्रारूढानि मायया।।
तमेव शरणं गच्छ सर्वभावने भारत!।
तत्प्रसादात्परां शान्तिं स्थानं प्राप्स्यसि शाश्वतम्।।[110]

"He from Whom is the emanation of beings, by Whom all this is pervaded, by worshipping Him in his own karma, man winneth perfection.

"Better is one's own dharma, though destitute of merits, than the well-executed dharma of another. He who doeth the karma laid down by his own nature incurreth not sin.

"Ishvara dwelleth in the hearts of all beings, O Arjuna, moving all beings by his Maya, as though mounted on a wheel.

"Flee unto Him for shelter with all thy being, O Bharata; by His grace thou shalt obtain supreme peace, the everlasting dwelling place.

वेदोऽखिलो धर्ममूलं स्मृतिशीले च तिद्वदाम्।
आचारश्चैव साधूनामात्मनस्तुष्टिरेव च।।[111]

''The whole of the Veda is the source of dharma; also the Smrit' and the character of those that know the Veda; also the conduct of the good and the satisfaction of the Self."

अष्टादशपुराणेषु व्यासस्य वचनद्वयम्।
परोपकारः पुरायाय पापाय परपीडनम्।।
यदन्यैर्विहितं नेच्छेदात्मनः कर्म पूरुषः।
न तत्परषेु कुर्वीत जानन्नप्रियमात्मनः।।
यद्यदात्मनि चेंच्छेत तत्परस्यापि चिन्तयेत्।
....

110 *Bhugavad-Gita,* xviii— 16. 47, 61. 62.

111 *Manusmriti,* ii—6.

यदन्येषां हितं न स्यादात्मनः कर्म पौरुषम्।
श्रपत्रंपत वायेन न तत्कुर्यात्कथचन॥
....
अतोयदात्मनोऽपथ्य परेषां न तदाचरेत्।

CHAPTER 4

THE STANDARD OF ETHICS

We have seen that the general standard by which actions should be judged at the present stage o£ evolution is Union, although many Jivas are not yet arrived at this stage. For the majority we can test each action by asking: Does it promote union? Does it promote separateness? If the answer to the first question is "Yes," the action is Right; if the answer to the second question is "Yes," the action is Wrong. This is why it was said in Chapter I. that morality showed men "how to live in harmony with each other and with their surroundings." To live in harmony is to promote union.

So also when Shri Krishna speaks of Divine and Asuric properties, we find that he classes as Divine those which promote union, and as Asuric those which promote separateness. "Fearlessness, cleanness of life, steadfastness in the yoga of wisdom, alms-giving, self-restraint and sacrifice and the study of the Shastras, austerity and straightforwardness, harmlessness, truthfulness, absence of wrath, renunciation, peacefulness, absence of crookedness, compassion to living beings, uncovetousness, mildness, modesty, absence of fickleness, vigour, forgiveness, fortitude, purity, absence of envy and pride."[112] Such virtues draw men together, and are based on the knowledge that all selves are one. On the other hand, see how those He marks as Asuric, the qualities which drive man apart, promote divisions: "Hypocrisy,

112 *Bhagavad-Gita,* xiv, 1—3.

arrogance and conceit, wrath and also harshness and unwisdom."[113] And his description of the Asuric type of man shews one who is full of ahamkara, egoism and selfishness.[114]

Let the young student then grasp firmly this distinction between Right and Wrong, and apply it to the guidance of his conduct. In later study he will add much to his thoughts on Right and Wrong, will learn many details, and have to solve many complexities; but this principle, this standard, will remain unaltered, for it is based on evolution, and is in accord with the will of Ishvara.

सवैषामपि चैतेषामात्मज्ञानं परं स्मृतम्।
तद्ध्यग्रंय सर्वविद्यानां प्राज्यते ह्यमृतं ततः॥
सर्वमात्मनि संपश्येत्सचासच समाहितः।
सर्वे ह्यात्मनि संपश्यन्नाधर्मे कुरुते मनः॥
आत्मैव देवताः सर्वाः सर्वमात्मन्यवस्थितम्।
....
एवंयः सर्वभूतेषु पश्यत्यात्मानमात्मना।
स सर्वसमतामेत्य ब्र ह्यमाभ्येति परं पदम्॥[115]

"Of all these things, the knowledge of the Self is the highest. It is the foremost of the sciences, for immortality is attained thereby.

"Let him with collected mind see in the Self both the Real and the Unreal. Thus beholding all in the Self, he turneth not his mind towards adharma.

"The Self is all the Devas; all resides in the Self. He who thus seeth the Self in all beings, by his own Self, he realiseth the equality of all and attaineth to the supreme state of Brahman."

113 Ibid, 4.

114 *Ibid*. 7—18.

115 *Manusmriti*, xii—85, 118, 119, 125.

CHAPTER 5

VIRTUES AND THEIR FOUNDATION

We have already seen that mutual sacrifice, another name for mutual service, is enjoined by the Sanatana Dharma, and it is easy to see that this is Right, since it promotes union. Thus the five daily sacrifices promote union between the sacrificer and Rishis, Devas, Pitris, Men and Amimals. Another way in which the Sanatana Dharma teaches us to do right is by explaining to us the three debts that we owe; the debt to the Rishis, paid chiefly in the Brahmacharya Ashrama, by study and by service of the teacher; the debt to the Pitris, the Ancestors, paid chiefly in the Garhasthya Ashrama, by rearing a family and by charity; the debt to the Devas, paid chiefly in the Vanaprastha Ashrama, by sacrifice and meditation.

A debt is something we owe; we have received and should repay. This payment of debt, of what is due, is called the discharge of duty, that which we owe to others, which we *ought* to do. The discharge of a duty is called a virtue; the non-discharge of a duty is called a vice. A virtuous man recognises his duties, his obligations, and fulfils them; a vicious man does not recognise nor fulfil them.

Virtues have also been called by Bhishma "forms of Truth,"[116] because Truth is that which is Real, is indeed, as Bhishma says, "the eternal Brahman."[117] Truth is the Divine Nature, and we see this in the reflection of Brahman that we call external Nature. Eor ail the laws of Nature are expressions of Truth, and work with perfect accuracy and changelessness. Now the greatest Truth of all is, as said before, the unity of the Self amidst the diversity of the

116 *Mahabharatam,* Shanti Parva—clxii.

117 *Ibid,* clxii.

Not-Self. All other truths and laws are such only because they are reflections, copies, of this great unity in diversity. Ana the form which this great Truth takes in. Ethical Science is that each one of us should feel for other selves as for himself, should feel himself to be the same as, or at least similar to, other selves; and, so feeling, we must always tell the truth, because to tell a falsehood to another is to regard him with distrust, to regard him as separate from, or even opposed to oneself, to prevent him from sharing with oneself in a common knowledge, which should be the same for all when all are as one. From the setting up of this separation by untruthfulness, consciously or unconsciously, endless harm results and vices arise. This description of the nature of virtues as forms of Truth corresponds again with our standard of Ethics, for truthfulness promotes union, while untruthfulness increases separateness.

Truthfulness has always been a marked characteristic of the noble characters described in Hindu literature. "My lips have never uttered an untruth," is a favourite phrase of the Heroes. Shri Krishna promised not to carry arms on Kurukshetra, and when He ran towards Bhishma with uplifted whip to help Arjuna, Arjuna refused His help because of His promise.[118] So also Yudhishthira, though almost despairing of victory, would not take His help, because of that same promise.[119] On the other hand, we read that when Yudhishthira for a moment in his utmost need forgot his truthfulness, and told a lie to the undoing of Drona. his war-chariot lost the power that upraised it from the earth and it sank to the ground.[120] When the Pandavas were yet in the forest, and Shri Krishna suggested that Yudhishthira might send an army against the Kurus, thus breaking the spirit of the promise that they would remain thirteen years in exile, Yudhishthira's answer was: "The

118 *Mahabharatam,* Bhishma Parva—lix,

119 *Ibid*

120 *Ibid*, Drona Parva—cciii.

sons of Pandu swerve not from the path of truth."[121] Even when loss follows, the pledged word must be kept. When Prahlada took the sovereignty of the three worlds from Indra, Indra disguised himself as a Brahmana and served him as his disciple. At last Prahlada was so pleased with him, that he offered to give him anything he asked for. Indra asked for Prahlada's "Shila," character, manner, behaviour, and Prahlada gave it, though he feared it meant his own ruin—as indeed it did—because he had pledged his word.[122]

And who can forget Bhishma's splendid answer, when his stepmother Satyavati prayed him to take the throne and marry, against his promise: 'I would renounce the three worlds, the empire of heaven or anything that may he still greater, but truth never will I renounce. Earth may renounce its scent, water may renounce its moisture, light may renounce its power of showing forms, the air may renounce its susceptibility to touch, the sun may renounce his glory, tire his heat, the moon his cool rays, space its capacity to generate sounds, the slayer of Vrittra his prowess, the God of justice his impartiality, but I renounce not truth."[123] Kama, the man of fire, the man of pride, the man of headlong straightforwardness, was born, the ancient story says, with a natural armour that no weapons could pierce through. The Devas, ever working that the cause of the Pandavas might prevail, were sorely anxious lest in the predestined combat between Karna and Arjuna, the latter should fail because of that strong armour. It was Kama's rule that he sat facing the east every day, studying the Vedas, till the sun turned the zenith, and he had vowed that during that period of his Veda-study every day, whatsoever a Brahmana asked of him that he had to give, he would give to him unfailingly; and one day Indra, the King of the Devas, seeing no other way, took on the sem-blance of an aged Brahmana and appeared before Karna and said he had a boon to ask. And

121 *Ibid,* Vana Parva—ciii.

122 *Mahabharatam,* Shanti Parva—cxxiv.

123 *Ibid,* Adi Parva-ciii.

Kama said that he would surely give it, if it were at all within his power. Then Indra said: "Give me this armour that you wear by nature on your body." Karna replied: "I know thee now to be no artless Brahmana, but the King of the Devas him self, disguised to help the cause of the Pandavas, But even the letter of my given word must be respected. Take what thou askest, though in giving thee thy wish I know I give my life, and what is even more than life to me, the only chance of conquering my soldier-rival, Arjuna, in battle !" And Karna hewed off that living armour piece by piece with his own hand and sword, and gave it all to Indra, winning thereby a longer life and a far nobler name than if he had defeated Arjuna.[124] King Dasharatha, of the Solar Race of Kings, asked by the Devas for help against the Asuras, battled against the latter as a Kshattriya should. His youngest wife, Kaikeyi, drove his war-chariot, and when the king sank into a swoon under his wounds, she skilfully bore him away on the chariot to a place of safety and preserved his life. For that deed the grateful King promised her two boons, which she put by for future need. Long afterwards, when the King was in his old age and wished to instal his eldest son, Rama, as the heir- apparent, she claimed the boons, and claimed them fearfully: Rama, eldest born and best beloved of the aged King, noblest of men, should wander forth into the forests as an exile, and the crown be placed on the head of Kaikeyi's son, Bharata. Dasharatha, knowing well that it was death to him to grant the boons, yet granted them and died. Better far that he should die, than that the King's word be broken, and truth slain.[125]

Bali, the Daitya king, had conquered Svarga and become unchallenged ruler of the three worlds. The rites of a great sacrifice, the sacred Ashvamedha, were spread out at his command. Vamana, Vishnu disguised as a dwarf, came to the sacrifice and begged as boon as much land as He could cover in three paces. Shukra,

124 *Mrhabharatam,* Vana Parva, ccoiii—cccix.

125 R*amayana*. Ayodhyukanda.

the preceptor of Bali, bade him refuse to carry out his gift, since Vamana was Vishnu. Bali answered: "The grandson of Prahlada shall never speak untruth. I will give to this Brahmana boy what I promised, even if he be Vishnu and my enemy." And when Vamana had covered the Triloki with two paces and demanded a third foothold, Bali offered his own head, and took as favour the loss of all his kingdom. And for this Vishnu blessed him, declaring: "His wealth gone, his position lost, himself overpowered and chained by enemies, forsaken by friends, reviled and cursed by his own preceptor Bali forsook not truth.'[126] The puranas say that for such acts of truth, by the blessing of Vishnu, Bali will be the next Indra, when the present Deva, whose proper name is Purandara, vacates that office (for Indra is the title of the great office of the sovereign of the divine kingdom, not a personal name).

As truth is Brahman, those who seek Brahman must be truthful. Above and beyond all else, therefore, a boy should strive for truthfulness.

जायमानो ब्राह्मणस्त्रिभिर्ऋणैर्ऋणवाजायतेयशेन देवेभ्यः
प्रजया पितृभ्यः स्वाध्यायेन ऋपिषभ्यः॥[127]

The Brahmana, being born, is horn a debtor with three debts; to the Devas by sacrifice, to the Ancestors by progeny, to the Rishis by study."

ऋणनि त्रीएयपाकृत्य मनो मोक्षे निवेशयेत्।
श्रनपाकृय मोक्षं तु सेवामानो व्रजत्यधः॥
श्रधीत्य विधिवद्वेदान् पुत्रांश्चोत्पाद्य धर्मतः।
इष्टा च शक्तितोयक्षैर्मनो मोक्षे निवेशयेत्॥[128]

126 *Vishnu-Bhagavata*, VIII, xv—xiii.

127 Veda text quoted by Kulluka in his commentary on *Manusmriti*,

128 *Manusmriti*, vi, 35—36.

"After having discharged the three debts let him turn his mind to Moksha. He who desireth Moksha, without having discharged them falleth downwards.

"Having studied the Vedas duly, having produced offspring lawfully, having offered sacrifices to the best of his power, let him turn to Moksha."

परस्परं भावयन्तः श्रेयः परमवाप्स्यथ॥
* * *
एवं प्रवर्तितं चक्रं नानुवर्त्तयतीहयः।
यघायुरिन्द्रियारामो मोघं पार्थ स जीवति॥[129]

"Nourishing one another ye shall reap the supremest good.

"He who on earth doth not follow the wheel thus revolving, sinful of life and rejoicing in the senses, he, O Partha, liveth in vain."

सत्यं सत्सु सदा धर्मः सत्यं धर्मः सनातनः।
सत्यमेव नमस्येत सत्यंहि परमा गतिः॥
सत्यं धर्मस्तपोयोगः सत्यं ब्रह्म सनातनम्।
सत्यंयज्ञः परः प्रोत्क्तः सर्वं सत्ये प्रतिष्ठितम्॥
* * *
सत्यं नामाव्यर्य नित्यमविकारि तथैव च।
सर्वधर्माविरुद्धेनयोगे नैतदवाप्यते॥
सत्यं च समता चैव दमश्चैव न संशयः।
श्रमात्सर्यं क्षमा चैव ह्रीस्तितिक्षाऽनसूयता॥
त्यागो ध्यानमथार्यत्वंघृतिश्च सततं दया।
अहिंसा चैव राजेन्द्र! सत्याकारास्त्रयोदश॥[130]

129 *Bhagavad-Gita,* iii, 11—16.

130 *Mahabhdratam,* Anushasans Parva c—lxii

"Truth is ever the (one) dharma of the good. Truth is the Sanatana Dharma. Bow only to the Truth. Truth is the final way. Truth is dharma, Truth is tapas. Truth is the eternal Brahman. Truth is the highest sacrifice, for all is founded on and upheld by Truth.

* * *

"Truth is the name of That which is Unperishing, Unchanging, Eternal. It is attained by the Yoga-meditation that opposeth not any Dharma.

"Truthfulness, equality (impartiality) self-control, absence of envious emulation, forgiveness, modesty, endurance, absence of jealousy, charity, thoughtfulness, disinterested philanthropy, selfpossession, and unceasing and compassionate harmlessness—these are the thirteen forms of Truth."

चत्वार एंकतो वेदाः साङ्गोपाङ्गाः सविस्तराः।
स्वधीता मनुजव्याघ्र सत्यमेकं किलैकतः॥[131]

"The four Vedas on the one side, well studied together with all their angas and upangas (are far out-weighed by) Truth alone on the other."

आत्मन्यपि न विश्वासस्तथा भवति सत्सुयः।
तस्मात्सत्सु विशेषेरा सर्वः प्रणयमिच्छति॥[132]

"Men place less trust in themselves than in the true. Hence all wish to secure the friendship of the true."

सतां सदा शारवतधर्मवृत्तिः।
सन्तो न सीदन्ति न च व्यथतिन्त।
सतां सन्द्रिर्पाफलः संगमोऽस्ति

131 *Mahabharatam*, Vana Parva I

132 Ibid—ccxci.

सद्भ्यों भयं नानुवर्त्तन्ति सन्तः।
सन्तो हि सत्येन नयन्ति सूर्य
सन्तो भूर्ति तपसा धारयन्ति।
सन्तो गतिर्भूतभव्यस्य राजन्
सतां मध्ये नावसीदन्ति सन्तः॥

"The true and the good act ever according to the Eternal Dharma. The true fail not, nor are cast down; never fruitless is contact with the true; the true feel no fear from the true. The true guide the Sun by the power of Truth; the true uphold the Earth by the power of self-denial. The true are the guides of the past and the future. O King, the true never suffer in the midst of the true."

(यतः प्रभवति) क्रोधः कामो वा भरतर्षभ।
शोकमोहौ विधित्सा च परासुत्वं च (तद्वद)॥
लोभो मात्सर्यमीर्ष्या च कुत्सा सूया कृपा भयम्।
* * *
त्रयोदशैतेऽतिबलाः शत्रवः प्राणिनां स्मृताः॥[133]

"Anger, lust, dejection, delusion, cynicism, wrongful activity, greed, envy, jealousy, irritated worry, sullen hate or malice, scorn and fear—these thirteen (vices and forms of untruth) O king, are the powerful enemies of living creatures."

यस्य विद्वान् हि वदतः क्षेत्रक्षो नामिङ्क्शते।
तस्मान्न देवाः श्रेयांसं लोकेऽनयं पुरुषं विदुः॥[134]

"The Devas know not a better being in the universe, than him of whom the all-knowing Witness feeleth no doubt when he speaketh."

---

133 *Mahabharatam,* Shanti Parva, xxsiii.

134 *Mansmriti,* viii—96

कर्मणयेवाधिकारस्ते मा फलेषु कदाचन।
मा कर्मफलहेतुर्भूर्ता ते सङ्गोऽस्तवकर्मरिा॥[135]

"Thy business is with the action only, never with its fruits; so let not the fruit of action be thy motive, nor be thou to inaction attached.

ऋंत सत्यं परं ब्रह्मल[136]

"The Supreme Brahman is the Right, is the Truth,"

CHAPTER 6

BLISS AND EMOTIONS

We have seen that Ishvara is Thought, Power and Bliss, and man, as His child, has also these characteristics. When the Jivatma becomes wrapped in dense matter, the aspect of his nature which is Bliss, is ever going outwards in search of satisfaction, trying to realise itself by uniting itself with the outer world. The impulses outwards are called desires, and when they unite the Jivatma to an object that gives him pleasure, so that he desires to be again united to such an object, the resulting emotion is called love, or liking. When, on the contrary, they unite the Jivatma, to an object that gives him pain, so that he desires to avoid union with such an object again, the resulting emotion is called hate, or dislike. The first makes an attraction between the Jivatma and the object; the second makes a repulsion.

The Jivatma thinks over these likes and dislikes, and gradually trains himself to direct his emotions rightly; emotions thus guided by reason in accordance with the will of Ishvara develop into Virtues, and thus the culture of the emotions forms the ethical

135 *Bhagavad-Gita,* ii—47.

136 *Nrisiottaratapini Upanishat,* i—6.

development of man. As he cultivates the emotion called love he unites himself to an ever-widening circle of beings, the family, the community, the nation, the race, loving them as himself and this love becomes a continually increasing expression of the Bliss aspect of his nature, which finds satisfaction in union.

We have seen that evolution is now leading us towards union, or, in other words, that the will of ishvara is guiding the separated selves towards union with each other and with Himself. In this union is Bliss; therefore the Right and the Happy are inseparable. Over and over again the Sanatana Dharma leads us to this one conclusion. "Brahman is bliss" therefore the Jivatma, being of the nature of Brahman, is also bliss, and unhappiness only arises when he goes against evolution, against the great Will, goes, in a word, wrong.

ब्रह्मैवेदं सर्वं सच्चिदानन्दरूपं
सच्चिदानन्दरूपमिदं सर्वम्।

"All this is Brahman—Sachchidananda; Sachchidananda is this all."

परिच्चखानि व्यतृणगत् स्वयंभू-
स्तस्मात्पराङ् पश्यति नान्तरात्मन्।

"The Self-born pierced the senses outwards; therefore (the Jiva) looketh outwards and not (towards) the inner Self."

यदा वै सुखं लभतेऽथ करोति नासुखं लब्ध्वा करोति
सुखमेव लब्ध्वा करोति...।
यो वै भूमा तत्सुखं नाल्पे सुखमस्ति भूमैव सुखम्
यत्र नान्यत्पश्यति नान्यच्छृणोति नान्यद्विजानाति
स भूमा श्रययत्राऽन्यत्पश्यत्यन्यच्छृरोत्यन्याद्विजानाति
तदल्पंयो वै भूमा तदमृतमथयदल्पं तन्मर्त्यं...।[137]

137 *Chhandogyopanishat,* VII, xxii—I; xiiii—1 slid xxiy—1.

"When (the Jiva) obtaineth pleasure, then he engageth in action; never doth he enter on action without having obtained pleasure; only when he hath obtained pleasure doth he engage in action.

"That which is infinite, that is (the true pleasure) happiness; there is no happiness in the finite. This infinite alone is happiness.

Where (the Self) seeth not another, heareth not another, knoweth not another (than the Self) that is the Infinite. Where (the Self) seeth, heareth, knoweth another (than the Self), that is the finite. That which is infinite is immortal; that which is finite is mortal."

सुखचैतन्यस्वरूपोऽपरिमितानन्दसमुद्रोऽविशिष्ट
सुख स्वरूपश्चानन्द इति।[138]

"Joy and consciousness, a limitless ocean of joy, than which there is no greater happiness—such is Ananda."

इष्टविषये बुद्धि। सुखबुद्धिरनिष्टविषये बुद्धिर्दुःखबुद्धिः।[139]

"The consciousness of pleasure is the consciousness of an object desired; the consciousness of pain is the consciousness of an object undesired."

सर्वाणि भूतानि सुखे रमन्ते
सर्वाणि दुःखस्य भृशं त्रसन्ते।।[140]

"All beings revel in pleasure; all shrink greatly from pain."

इच्छाद्वेषसमुत्थेन द्वन्द्वमोहेन भारत!।
सर्वभूतानि संमोहं सर्गेयान्ति परन्तप।।[141]

138 *Sarvataropanishat.*

139 *Mahvbharatam,* Shilnti Parva ccxxxi.—327.

140 *Bhagavad-Gita,* vii— 27

141 *Ibid,* xiii—6.

"By the delusion of the pairs of opposites, O Bharata, sprung from attraction and repulsion, O slayer of foes, all beings walk this world, wholly deluded."

इच्छा द्वेषः सुखं दुःख सङ्घातश्चेतना धृतिः।
एंत्तक्षेत्रं समासेन सविकारमुदाहृतम्॥[142]

"Desire, aversion, pleasure, pain, the compound (organism), intelligence, firmness, these, briefly described, constitute the Field and its changes."

काम एषं क्रोध एष रजोगुणासमुन्द्रवः।

"It is Kama (desire) and it is Krodha (anger), arising out of Rajas."

इन्द्रियस्योन्द्रियस्यार्थे रागद्वेषौ व्यवस्थितौ।[143]
तयोर्न वशमागच्छत्तौ ह्यास्य परिपन्थिनौ॥

"Affection and aversion for the objects of sense abide in the senses; let none come under the dominion of these two; they are obstructors of the path."

रागद्वेवियुत्त्केस्तु विष्यानिन्द्रियेश्चरन्।[144]
श्रात्मवश्वैर्विधेयात्मा प्रसांदमधिगच्छति॥

"But the disciplined self, moving among sense objects with senses free from attraction and repulsion, mastered by the self, goeth to peace."

---

142 *Ibid,* iii—87.

143 *Bhagavad- Gitia,* iii—34.

144 Ibid, ii—64.

यः शास्त्रविधिमुत्सृज्य वर्तते कामकारतः।
न स सिद्धिमवाप्नेत न सुखं न परां गतिम्॥[145]

"He who, having cast aside the ordinances of the Shastras, followeth the promptings of desire, attaineth rot to perfection, nor happiness, nor the highest goal."

एको वशी सर्वभूतान्तरात्मा
एकरूपं वहुधायः करोति।
तमात्मस्थंयेऽनुपश्यन्ति धीरा-
स्तेषां सुखं शा श्वंत नेतरेषाम्॥ल[146]

"The One Who controlleth all, the inmost Self of all beings, Who maketh many forms of one form—they who see That One in the Self, only to those rulers of intelligence belongeth the Eternal Happmess, u none else."

CHAPTER 7

SELF-REGARDING VIRTUES

We have seen that the Jivatma is related to all around him, and that Ethics is concerned with making his relations with others harmonious. But we must not forget that he is most closely related to his own koshas, or bodies, the parts of the Not-Self that he has most closely united to himself, and that unless he is in harmonious relations with these, he can hardly hope to be in harmonious relations with the bodies that are further away from him. While he is young, these bodies of his master him, and lead him into all sorts

145 *Ibid,* xvi—23.

146 *Kathopanishat.,* y—12.

of trouble; as he grows older, he begins to try to master them, and many a hard tight he has with them, before he develops the great virtue called self- control—the control of the lower selves by the higher Self, of the bodies by the Jivatma. Virtues that belong to these bodies, considered by themselves, rather than in connection with the relations between different Jivatmas, are called self-regarding in modern classifications. But every one can see that a person who has these virtues will promote harmonious relations with others much more than one who has them not.

Manu, the great law-giver, lays much stress on the necessity for this self-control, and gives some most valuable advice about it. He says that action has three forces behind it, and that each of these must be mastered. "Action is born of mind, speech and body. "[147]

The mind—the Manomayakosha, which includes the emotions—must be conquered. This is the hardest task of all. For the mind runs after the objects of desire, swayed and controlled by the longings to possess the objects which promise to, give pleasure. The emotions are ever craving satisfaction, and the mind seeks to gratify them, becoming their slave. The Jivatma must free the mind from this slavery, and subdue it for his own service, making it the master of the senses and the sense-organs: as Manu says: "In conquering this (the mind) the two sets of five become conquered."[148] The "two sets of five" are the ten Indriyas, that is, the five Jnanendriyas and the five Karmendriyas.

Let the student, then, aim at ruling his mind; if it runs to evil things let him call it hack; let him allow it to fix Itself only on good things. This is the first, the most difficult, the most essential part of self-control.

The control of speech is the next step; we must think before we speak. Hasty speech leads us into endless troubles. Arjuna was often very hasty in his speech, and so got himself into

---

147 Loc, cit., xi—13

148 Loc, cit., xi—02.

many difficulties; as in his hasty vow to slay himself if he did not kill Jayadratha, the slayer of his son, before sunset, thus necessitating the interference of Shri Krishna, who shrouded the sun prematurely to induce Jayadratha to come out from his shelter.[149] So again in his quarrel with Yudhishthira, provoked by Yudhishthira's taunting speech,[150] and on other occasions. Nay, his failure to keep a hasty vow led to his death on the Great Journey: "Arjuna said he would consume all our foes in a single day. Proud was he in bis heroism, but he did not what he boasted. Hence has he fallen downd."[151] He who has conquered his tongue is near to self-mastery.

Thirdly, the physical body must be controlled, and not be allowed to hurry us into sin. for its gratification. Says Shri Krishna: "Worship of the Devas, the twice-horn, the gurus and the wise, purity, straightforwardness, chastity and harmlessness, are called the austerity of the body."[152] Youth is the time for conquering the body, for it is then most easily subdued, and set in the right way. For the body is a creature of habit and though at first, it will oppose the will of the Jivatma with great energy, a little perseverance makes it give way, and then it goes as contentedly and readily along the new road as it did along the old.

Among the sources of evil and of sorrow that we should strive to get rid of by this self-control is selfish desire, for out of the Insatiable desire for material wealth and material pleasures grow many miseries, and peace arises from the absence of these desires and not by their continued gratification. Thus Manki found. For, greedy of wealth, Manki had searched for it long, but ever he seemed doomed to disappointment. With the last remnant of his property he bought a pair of calves to train up for the plough. But

149 *Mahabharatam,* Drona Parva.

150 *Ibid,* Karna Purva. Ixx—ixx.

151 I*dib,* Mahaprasthanika Parva.

152 *Bhagavad-Gita,* xvii—14.

fate ordained that the cord with which the two were tied should get entangled with a passing camel, so that both were killed. This last mischance opened the heart of Manki, so that desire fled thence unconfined, and Manki burst forth into song: "He that desires happiness must renounce desire. Well did Shuka say that of these two—the one who gets all that he wishes and the one who casts off every wish—the latter, who renounces all, is surely much superior to the former, for none can ever attain to the end of all desires. Do thou, O my soul, so long a slave to greed, taste now for once the joys of freedom and tranquillity. Long have I slept, but I shall sleep no longer; I shall wake. No more shalt thou deceive me, O Desire. Whatever object thou didst fix my heart on, that didst thou force me to follow, heedless, never pausing to enquire if it were easy or impossible to gain. Thou art without intelligence. Thou art a fool. Ever unsatisfied, thou burnest like a fire, always lambent for more offerings. Thou art impossible to fill, like pace itself. Thy one wish is to plunge me into sorrow. This day we part. From this day, O Desire, I live no longer in thy company. I think no more of thee or of thy train. I cast thee off, with all the. passions of my heart. I, who was harassed with despair before, have now a attained to perfect peace of mind. In full contentment of the heart, senses at ease, shall I live henceforth on what comes to me, and labour no more fur the satisfaction of thy wishes, O my foe. Casting off thee and all thy train, I gain at once instead tranquillity and self-restraint, forgiveness and compassion and deliverance." Thus Manki lost a little, and gained all.[153]

Hear also the story of King Yayati, who driven mad by wild desire, took from his own son his fair and splendid youth to strive to fill therewith the lever-gaping maw of Desire the insatiable. For thus the story runs.

King Yayati, son of Nahusha, of the Lunar Dynasty of Kings, was over-fond of the pleasures of sense and fell into sin, which

153 *Mahabharatam,* Shanti Parva—clxxvii

brought upon him the wrath of his father-in-law, the great Rishi Shukra, the priest of the Titan-Kings. Because of that wrath, King Yayati was suddenly struck with shrivelled and tottering old age in the very midst of his glorious prime of manhood. He propitiated the Rishi, and Shukra, taking pity on him, decreed that he could exchange, for a thousand years, his age and feebleness for the health and youth of any of his sons, who should consent willingly to the exchange. Yayati asked his five sons in succession; the fifth and youngest Puru, for love and reverence of his father, gave him his own youth and took from him his age for the period of a thousand years. For that long period King Yayati assiduously pursued the pleasures of the senses, endeavouring to exhaust the luxuries of the world of matter. But ever he found that his craving grew, even when his senses dulled with satiation. He longed in vain that his longing for the world of sense should be exhausted by fulfilment. As one spoke of a wheel running after another spoke of it, the chase was endless. At the last, as the thousand years approached their close, a great vairagya arose in his mind, and he saw that desire ceases not with satisfaction but with frustration. He called Puru to him, took back his own old age with gladness, and gave to him his youth together with the kingdom, and retired into the forests chanting the verse that summed up all his life-experience:

"Desire may not be quenched by enjoyment of its objects; it only increases manifold therewith, as fire with libations of butter."[154]

Let us pause a moment on the word "harmlessness," in the above quotation of Shri Krishna's words, "Harmlessness is the highest Dharma," Bhishma taught. We should injure nothing. Our life should he a source of help, not of harm. The control of the body includes this abstention from injuring others. As said Brihaspati: "That man who practises the religion of universal

154 *Mahabharatam,* Anushasana Parva, cxvi—37.

compassion, achieves the highest good....One should never do that to another which one regards as injurious to one's own self. This, in brief, is the rule of righteousness. "[155]

People often harm others in more thoughtlessness, and so bring about much trouble. When Yudhishthira and Duryodhana and their brothers were boys and all lived and studied together, Bhima, who was the strongest of them all, often indulged in practical jokes and rough horse-play, exercising his great strength with boyish thought-lessness upon the younger and weaker boys. When a number of them climbed up into a tree to pluck the fruit, he would take the trunk between his hands and shake the tree, till the little bovs tumbled down like ripe fruits. Bhima thought it was great fun and laughed; hut some of the boys were hurt, hurt in body, and what was worse, hurt in mind. Again, when they were out bathing and swimming in the river that flowed beneath the walls of Hastinapura, Bhima would swim underneath the other boys, and, catching hold of a number of them, would dive into the water, and hold them there till they were almost drowned, while his own greater lung-capacity helped him efficiently against similar distress. He delighted in this, but the others were agonised. What was the consequence? A smouldering fire of repulsion and dislike, that later on grew into a blazing fire of hate that consumed Kaurava and Pandava alike. The boyish thoughtlessness of Bhima was one of the chief causes of the Great War. It is true that unless the combustibles are there, the spark will not kindle the fuel; unless the tissues are tainted, the microbe will not develop the disease; still it is our duty to guard against such a destructive spark, such a death-bringing microbe, as long and as cearfully as we can. When thoughtless exercise of strength hurts the weak who cannot retaliate, then the anger, that is born but is not vented, becomes transformed into what is contemptuously called hate and malice, but is in

155 *Ibid*—cxiii.

reality far less to blame than the careless spoliation of the weaker by the stronger. To the superficial eye of one who is himself equally inclined in his secret mind to oppression, such acts may appear blameless or even magnificent. But to the just eye of a true chivalry they will always appear in their real character of meanness and tyranny. And he who studies the Great History carefully knows well that the Pandavas were not all to praise, nor the Kauravas all to blame.

The triple control of mind, speech and body results in righteousness, in right character expressing itself in right conduct. The man who has thus put himself into right relations with the things nearest to him. his own emotions, mind and body, and has thus partially acquired the virtues classified as "self-regarding" or "egoistic" in western ethical boobs, is able to practise more effectively those classified therein as "altruistic," those which arise in relation to other living beings.

We have now to study the virtues and vices which arise in the relations between human beings. These are best classified under three heads:

1. The virtues and vices which arise in relation to superiors.
2. The virtues and vices which arise in relation to equals.
3. The virtues and vices which arise in relation to inferiors.

In this way we shall obtain a clear and simple classification of the virtues which make our relations with all around us harmonious, and seeing them distinctly, we can strive to attain them. And we shall also see plainly the vices which make disharmony and can try to avoid them. All the virtues have their root in pure Love, and have Bliss for their fruit; all the vices have their root in personal Hate, and their fruit is Misery.

शुभाशुफलं कर्म मनोवागदेहसम्भवम्।
कर्मजा गतयो नृणमुत्तमाधममध्यमाः॥

* * *

मानस्त्रं मनसैवायमुपभुङ् के शुभाशुभभ्।
वाचा वाचा कृंत कर्म कायेनैव तु कायिकम्।
* * *
वाग्दएडोयऽथ मनोदणडः कर्मदराडस्तथैव च।
यस्यैते निहिता बुद्धौ त्रिदएडीति से उच्यते।।
त्रिदएडमेतन्निक्षिप्य सर्वभूतेषु मानवः।
कामक्रोधौ तु संयम्य ततः सिद्धिं निगच्छति।।[156]

"Karma, that bringeth good or evil fruit, ariseth in the mind, or in speech, or in the body, And threefold are the paths of men, according to their karma, high or low or middling.

* * *

"This (Jiva) reapeth good or evil, mental with the mind, vocal with speech, and bodily even with the body.

* * *

"The danda of the speech, the danda of the mind, the danda of the act—he who has laid these rods (of ruley over his intelligence he is the Tridandi.

"Having laid these rods (of control over his mind) with respect to all beings, and having conquered lust and anger, (the Jiva) attaineth perfection.

देवद्विजगुरुप्राक्षपूजनं शोचमार्जवम्।
ब्रह्मचर्यमहिंसा च शारीरं तप उच्बतें।।
भनुद्वेगकरं वाक्यं सत्यं प्रिबहितं चयत्।
रुवाध्यायाभ्यसनं चैथ वाङ्मय तप उच्यते।।
मनः प्रसादः सौम्यत्वं मौनमात्मविनिप्रहः।
भावसंशुद्धिरित्येतत्तपो मानसमुच्यते।।[157]

---

156 *Manusmriti,* xii—3, 4, 8,10, II.

157 *Bbnoarad-Gita,* xvii—14,15, 16,

"Worship given to the Devas, to the twice-born, to the teachers and to the wise, purity, straightforwardness, continence and harmlessness—are called the austerity of the body.

"Speech causing no annoyence, truthful and beneficial, the practice of the study of the Scriptures, are called the austerity of Speech.

"Mental happiness, equilibrium, silence, self-control, purity of nature—this is called the austerity of the mind."

न जातु कामः कामानामुपभोगेन शाम्यति।
हविषा कृणावर्त्त्मेव भूय एवाभिवर्धते॥[158]

"Not by the enjoyment of the objects of desire doth desire abate; rather it increaseth again, as fire with libations of butter."

श्रसंशयं महावाहो मनो दुर्निग्रहं चतम्।
अम्यासेन तु कौन्तेय वैराग्येण च गृह्यते॥
यतोयतो निश्चरति मनश्च्चलमस्थिरम्।
ततस्ततो नियम्यैदतदात्मन्येव वशं नयेत्॥[159]

"Without doubt, O mighty-armed, the mind is hard to curb and restless. But, O son of Kunti, it may be curbed by constant practice and by dispassion.

"As often as the wavering and unsteady mind, goeth forth, so often, reining it in, let him bring it under the control of the Self."

अभ्यासेऽयसमर्थोसि मत्कर्मपरमो भव।
मद्र्थमपि कर्माणि कुर्वन् सिद्धिमवाप्स्यसि॥[160]

---

158 *Mahabharatam*, Anushasan Parva, cxvi—37.

159 *Bbnoarad-Gita,* iv, 35—26.

160 *Ibid, xii—10.*

"If also thou art not equal to constant practice, be intent on My service. Performing actions for My sake, thou shalt attain perfection."

नित्यो नित्याना चेतनश्चेतनानां
एको बहूनांयो विद्धाति फामान्।
तभात्मस्थंयेऽनुपश्यन्ति धीरा-
स्तेषां शान्तिः शा श्वती नेतरेषाम्।।[161]

"That which is the Eternal of all eternals, That which is the Life of all lives, That which being One inspireth many with desires—the wise that behold that One seated within themselves, to them alone belongs the lasting peace, unto none else."

गोत्रजः सहजशत्रुरित्यसौ
नीतिरस्तु धनलोभदुर्धियाम्।
वृद्धतुस्यलघुपुंवृत जगद-
धीधनस्य पितृमित्रपुत्रवत्।।[162]

"The kinsman is the congenital foe—such is the view of those whose minds are blinded by the greed of wealth. To him whose wealth is wisdom, the world, that is filled With his elders, equals and youngers, is (as a world of) parents, friends and children."

श्रविजित्यय आत्मानममात्सान् विजिगीषते।
अवित्रान्वाऽजितामात्यः सोऽवशःपरिर्हायते।।
श्रात्मानमे प्रथम द्वेषरूपरेणयोजयेत्।
ततोऽमात्यानमित्रांश्र न मोघं विजिगीषते।।[163]

---

161 *Kathopanishad* v—13.

162 *Muhabharitam,* Udyoga Tarva, ii—17.

163 *Ibid,* oxxviii, 20—30.

"He that, without having conquered himself, wisheth to conquer his ministers, or that, without having conquered his ministers, wisheth to conquer his foes, he faileth helplessly.

"But he that conquereth himself first, as his own foe, and thereafter conquers his ministers and his foes, (his work) is not vain.

धर्मस्य विधयो नैकेये वे प्रोक्ता मनीषिभिः।
स्वं स्वं विज्ञानमाश्रित्य दमस्तेषां परायणाम्॥
दमं निःश्रेयसे प्राहुर्वृद्धा निश्चित दर्शिनः।
ब्राह्मणस्य विशेषेण दमों धर्मः सनातनः।
श्रदान्तः पुरूपः क्लेशमभीक्ष्णं प्रतिपद्यते।
श्रनर्थाश्र बहूनन्यान् प्रसृजत्यात्मदोषजान्॥
आश्रमेषु चतुर्वाहुर्दममवोत्तमं व्रतम्।
तस्य लिङ्गानि वक्ष्यामियेषां समुदयो दमः।
क्षमा धृतिरहिंसा च समता सत्यमार्जवम्।
इन्द्रियाभिजयो दाक्ष्र्य मार्दवं ह्रिचापलम्॥
श्रकार्परायमसंरम्भः सन्तोषः प्रियवादिता।
अविहिंसानसूया चाप्येषां समुदयों दमः॥

"Not one (but many are) the branches of dharma that have been declared by the wise, each resting upon his own knowledge. But Dama (self-control) is the basis of them all.

"The elders, the seers of the sure, have declared that Dama leadeth to the Highest; especially for the Brahmana is Dama the (whole of) Sanatana Dharma.

"The man that is not self-controlled meeteth suffering everywhere; and many troubles he causeth, all arising out o£ his own defects.

"For all the four Ashrumas, Dama is the highest vow. I shall declare to thee the marks thereof, the characteristics of which Dama is the source:

"Forgiveness, self-possession, harmlessness, equability, truthfulness, straightforwardness, the conquest of the senses, skill, gentleness, modesty, restfulness, absence of scorn, absence of excitement, sweet speech, harmlessness, and absence of jealousy—of all these is self-control the source."

धृतिः क्षमा दमोऽस्तेयं शौचमिन्द्रियनिग्रहः।
धीर्विद्या सत्यमक्रोधो दशकं धर्मलक्षणम्॥[164]

"Self-possession, patience, self-control, integrity, purity, restraint, intelligence, learning, truthfulness, absence of anger—these ten are the marks of dharma.'

अहिंसा सत्यमस्तेंय शौचमिन्द्रियनिग्रहः।
एंत सामासिकं धर्मं चातुर्वणर्येऽब्रवीन्मनुः॥[165]

"Harmlessness, truth-speaking, refraining from theft, control of the senses—such is the essence of the dharma that Manu declared for all the four castes."

सत्यमस्तेमक्रोधो ह्रीः शौचं धीर्धृतिर्दमः।
संयतेन्द्रिता विद्या धर्मः सर्व उदहृतः[166]

"Truthfulness, absence of theft, absence of anger, modesty, purity, intelligence, self-possession, self-control, restraint of the senses, learning—this is declared to be the whole of dharma."

164 *Manusmriti,* vi—93.
165 *Ibid,* x—63.
166 *Yajiiaralkya,* iii—66.

CHAPTER 8

VIRTUES AND VICES IN RELATION TO SUPERIORS

Love which is unselfish prompts us to make sacrifices for others, and to restrain ourselves for the common good; therefore such love is the root of virtues, of the qualities that promote union. So also hate prompts us to take from others, to grasp at all desirable things for our own separate enjoyment to the injury of others; therefore hate is the root of vices, of the qualities that promote separateness. Moreover, when we make a sacrifice for one we love, we feel happiness in making it, and we thus learn that the deepest happiness, real bliss, lies in giving, which is the joy of the Jivatma, and not in taking, which is the joy of the bodies.

Let us see how love impels a man to act in relation to his superiors, to those to whom he looks up. A man's superiors are: God, Sovereign, Parents, Teachers, and the Aged.

Love to God shows itself as *Reverence, Devotion*, *Worship* and *Submission* to His Will. We find all lovers of God show these virtues. See how Bhishma reverences and worships Shri Krishna, the Avatara of Vishnu: at the Rajasuya sacrifice of Yudhishthira Bhishma bids them offer the first arghya to Him, and Narada declares that "He who approveth not the worship offered unto Krishna, the oldest One in the universe, deserveth neither soft words nor consideration. Those men that will not worship Krishna, with eyes like lotus- petals, should be regarded as dead though moving."[167] And so also, when Bhishma lay dying, he was thinking "of Krishna in mind, word and act," and his one thought

167 *Mahahharatam,* Sabha Parva, xixviii—8.

was to receive His blessing;[168] he closed the great exhortation with the recital of "the thousand names of Vasudeva," and his last words, ere bidding all farewell, asked Shri Krishna's permission to depart.[169]

In Parhlada, the son of the Daitya King Hiranyakashipu, we have one of the most famous examples of devotion. Despite all his teachers could say, he steadily prayed to and praised Hari. In vain did his father threaten him and seek to kill him; the wild elephant who should have trampled on him failed to injure; the rocks that should have crushed him lay light as down on his bosom; the sword that should have struck off his head fell blunted from his neck; the poison that should have curried death along his veins proved harmless as water; and at last Narasimha, the Avatara, burst from the granite pillar, and delivered Hari's servant from the tyrant who sought to slay.[170]

Dhruvy, leaving his father's palace to dee from the unkindness of his step-mother, shows such fervour of devotion and such courage and steadfastness in worship, that Hari appears to him, and gives him as throne the pole-star, on the boundary of the Triloki, whereon he lives and reigns.[171]

Nothing, perhaps, is more marked in the perfect human character of Ramchnndra, than His unwavering submission to the Divine Will. Over and over again during the whirl that followed His sudden exclusion from the throne, He calms those around Him by reminding them that all that happens is by the good law, and He Himself is utterly unshaken by the storm, knowing the Real amid all changing unrealities.

On the other hand, we read constantly of the overthrow of those who do not honour the Supreme Lord. Mighty rulers like Ravana, who was monarch in Lanka, fell because they thought themselves

168 *Ibid,* Shanti Parva

169 Ibid, Anushisaua Parva.—cxlix.

170 Bee *Vishnu Parana,* I, xvi—xx.

171 See ibid, I, xi—xii,.

rivals of ishvara, and set themselves against His loving will for the worlds.[172] Jarasandha, the King of Magadha, refusing, though hidden by Shri Krishna, to set free the Kings he had captured was slain by Bhima; Shishupale fell before the discus of the Lord he denied;[173] Duryodhana perished, with his friends and followers, for his persistent rejection of Shri Krishna's counsels;[174] the list might be extended for many pages. Out of all these shines out the warning that those who show hate to Ishrara must perish.

Loyalty to the Head of the State is equally insisted on in the Shastras, not only by direct command but by example. When Yudhishthira is King in Indraprastha, and his four brothers go out to war, they bring to his feet all the wealth they gained; they fought for their King, not for themselves.[175] So when Yudhishthira was exiled after the gambling-match, and the people came out to follow him, leaving their allegiance to Dhritarashtra, the loyal prince bade them return to Hastina- pura and obey their proper ruler, since only thus could they secure the general prosperity.

This loyalty was fostered in the people by the devotion to duty imposed on the King, and by the high ideal of kingship insisted on. Utatthya, of the race of Angira, instructing the King Mandhata, son of Yuvanashva, said:—"One becometh a King in order that he may uphold righteousness, and not that he may conduct himself capriciously. The King is the protector of the world, O Mandhata ! If he act righteously, he attaineth to the honours of a veritable God upon earth. But if he act unrighteously he sinketh into hell. All creatures rest upon righteousness; and righteousness, in turn, resteth upon the King. That King alone is a true King who upholdeth righteousness. If he fail to chastise unrighteousness, the Devas desert his mansions, and he incurreth obloquy among men."

---

172 *Ramdyana,* Yuildhakandam.

173 *Makabhara'am*, Shalya, Parva—xx

174 *Ibid*—xi.

175 *Ibid,* Sabha Parva, xxv-xxxiii,

Patriotism, the love of one's country, and *Public Spirit,* caring for the nation more than for oneself, are virtues that are so closely akin to loyalty that they should never be separated from it. "King and Country" are the object of true loyalty. No man should be without this love of country and the readiness to sacrifice himself for his native land; for national greatness cannot exist without patriotism and public spirit, and national greatness means, in the long run, family and individual prosperity: the whole and the part cannot be separated. Public spirit makes a man feel the successes and the sufferings of his country as though they were his own—as indeed they are. It makes him try to protect the weak from injustice, to resist wrong, to uphold the law, to stand for justice, to refuse to make unfair profit at the cost of the community or to cheat it by evading what is due to it from himself. The heroes of ancient India are constantly described as "intent on the welfare of others Shri Krishna bids Arjuna see "to the protection of the masses," to "the maintenance of mankind." The man who thinks only of himself and of his family is short-sighted, and is really undermining his and their future happiness.

To Parents is due ever the most complete *Obedience*, and this is one of the most often- repeated injunctions of the Sanatana Dharma. See how Ramachandra, the Great Example, obeys his father. When Dasharatha is inveigled into granting Rama's exile and the son is told by Kaikeyi that His father fears to speak his will: "Speak, O honoured lady, the desire of the King," is His quick reply, "and I will carry it; out There is no service greater than service of the father, than carrying out his words." And to all arguments counselling resistance, He gives the steadfast answer: "There is no power in me to transgress my father's order I shall abide by my father's orders." And later, when His father was dead, and Bharata, most unwilling regent, held His crown in trust, all His answer to Bharata's passionate pleadings that He should ascend the throne was that His father had sent Him to the forest, and had placed Bharata on the throne; each must do his own task, according to the father's word: "What My father hath commanded must not be made untrue."

Again we read in the *Mahabharatam* the story of the knower of Brahman, shrouded in the impure body of a fowler, who led to his parents the Brahmana Kaushika, who came to learn wisdom at his feet. The fowler took the Brahmana to the beautiful rooms in which he had housed his aged parents, saying that his own happy state of knowledge and peace was due to his filial piety; having bowed low at their feet he introduced his guest and then told him: "These my parents are the idols that I worship; whatever is due to the Devas I do to them...To me they are like the three sacred fires mentioned by the learned; and, O Brahmana, they seem to me to be as good as sacrifices, or the four Vedas,..The two parents, the sacred fire, the soul, and the guru, these five, O good Brahmana, are worthy of the highest reverence." He then told Kaushika that he had acted wrongly in leaving his parents in his anxiety to learn the Vedas, and that he should go back to them and console them: "Return to the side of thy father and mother, and be diligent in honouring thy parents, for I do not know if there be any virtue higher than this."[176]

Who does not know how Bhishma won the boon, that Death should not touch him until he himself permitted it, by resigning throne and marriage to win for his father the bride for whom, in silence, the father's heart was yearning? King Shantanu, of the lunar race of Kings, wished to marry the beautiful Satyavati, but struggled against himself for the sake of his son Bhishma. A step-mother, he thought, might not be kind to his beloved son. The care born of the struggle showed on King Shantanu's face, and Bhishma made enquiry of the ministers and learned the cause. He went to the father of Satyavati and asked that she be married to the King. The father said: "The King is aged; thou shalt shortly

176 M*akabharatam,* Vana Parva, ccxiii—ccxv.

reign in his stead. I would rather marry my daughter to thee." But Bhishma replied: "Say not such a thing. When my father has wished to marry her, she is my mother already; give her to the King.'' Then Satvavati's father said: "But I shall do so only if her son succeeds the King in sovereignty." Bhishma said at once: "I promise to forego my birth-right. I shall place that younger brother of mine upon the throne." But Satyavatl's father said again: "We know thy word once given may not be broken. But what shall bind thy sons from disputing their uncle's right?" Then Bhishma said: "I promise never to marry at all; so there shall be no sons to me who may dispute their uncle's right Now do thou let my father have his wish." And because of his fearful promises the Devas cried out with a bodiless voice: "He has been known as Devavrata so long; he shall now be known as Bhishma—the Terrible"—terrible surely to himself but most loved and most dear to all true Hindu hearts. King Shantanu too, when he heard that the vows had been already made and could not now be helped, took Satyavat- to wife; but in the fulness of his father's love bestowed on Bhishma the gift of death at his own will alone. Men that prevail over their passions thus, and can conserve their manhood perfectly, may well prevail against the might of death itself, long as they like.

On the other hand, it was Duryodhana's stub-born insolence and disobedience to his parents that precipitated the war which destroyed his house. Over and over again his father pleaded with him to yield to the just demands of the Pandavas, and give them a share in their ancestral property, but Duryodhana scorned his prayers and persisted in his own way. Even when his mother, Gandhari, begged him in open sabha to obey his father and to regard his duty, he treated her harshly and disrespectfully, and so brought on his head the doom of failure. No son can succeed who grieves his father or mother by disobedience or by disrespect.

The Teacher is added to the Father and Mother by the Sanatana Dharma, as the third great object of reverence and service, and we see this virtue also in the ancient heroes who should serve as examples to all Hindu boys. How deep is the love, how unfailing the reverence, shown by the Pandavas to Bhishma, to Drona, even when compelled to fight against them; see them bowing at their teacher's feet ere the battle joins on Kurukshetra; and when Dhristadyumna seized the white lucks of Drona, hear the agonised cry of Arjuna: "Bring the teacher alive! do not slay him ! he should not be slain!" and his heart-broken sob when the crime is complete: "I have sunk into hell, overcome with shame."

The only valid reason for disobedience to the Guru is held to lie. in the Sanatana Dharma, in previous promise or clear duty. Bhishma, the example of dharma, gives a striking illustration of this in his career. After the death of his father Shantanu, Bhishma, in accordance with his vow, placed his younger brother Chitrangada on the throne, and when Chitrangada was slain in battle, then he placed the second brother Vichitravirya on the throne of Hastinapura. Looking for suitable wives for Vichitravirya, Bhishma heard that the three daughters of the King of Kashi were about to hold a Svayamvara, and were in all respects worthy of marriage with his brother. He. went to Kashi, and by Lis sole might in battle carried them off from the midst of the assembled candidates for their hands. When he brought them to Hastinapura the younger two, Ambika and Ambalika, willingly consented to marry Vichitravirya; but the eldest, Amba, said she wished to marry Shalva, King of another country, having chosen him for husband long before.[177] Bhishma sent her with all honour to King Shalva; but he sent her back saying she had been won in battle from him and he could not take her back as a gift. Then Amba said to Bhishma: "If Shalva will not marry me, because you won me from him in battle, then you must marry me yourself." Bhishma was greatly distressed for her sake, but in view of his vow of lifelong celibacy could not consent. Then Amba

177 *Mahabharatam,* Adi Parva, c.

was very angry and went to Bhishma's Guru Parashurama; and Parahurama sided with her and ordered Bhishma to marry Amba. But he declined, deeming the keeping of his vow a higher duty than obedience to his teacher in a wrongful order. And ultimately there was a great battle between Parashurama and Bhishma. For many days the single combat lasted, and many wounds were received by both; and more than once they fainted with fatigue and loss of blood and shock of serious wound: but reviving again, they renewed the fight, till on the twenty-eighth day, the aged Parashurama acknowledged that he could do no more; and Bhishma won his cause. Yet because however unwillingly, he had brought much sorrow upon Amba, karma decreed that she should prove the means of his death.

Reverence to the Aged fitly closes the list of virtues which should flower when we come into relation with our superiors, and it was one of the marked characteristics of the ancient Hindu character. The wisdom which is the fruit of long experience is the precious treasure in possession of the aged, and they willingly pour this forth for the benefit of the teachable, courteous, respectful youth. In the hurry of modern life, this respect for the aged is apt to be trampled under foot, and it is the more necessary that care should be taken to cultivate it.

नयुज्यमानया भक्तया भगवत्यखिलात्मनि।
सदृशोऽस्ति शिवः पन्थायोगिनां ब्रह्मसिद्धये।।
ज्ञानवैराग्ययुक्तेन भक्तियुक्तेन चात्मना।
परिपश्यत्युदासीन प्रकृतिं च हतौजसम्।।
सतां प्रसङ्गान्मम वीर्यसंविदो
भवन्ति हत्कर्णारसायनाः कथाः।
तज्जोपणादा श्वपवर्गवर्त्मनि
श्रद्धा रतिर्भक्तिणनुक्रमिध्यति।।

भक्तया पुमान् जातविराग ऐन्द्रियाद्
दृष्टश्रुतान्मद्रचनानुचिन्तया।
चित्तस्ययत्तो ग्रहणोयोगयुक्तो-
यतिष्यते ऋजुभिर्वोगमार्गैः॥
भ्रसेवायऽयं प्रकृतेर्गुरानां
ज्ञानेन वैराग्य विजृम्भितन।
योगेन मय्यर्पितया च भक्तथा
मां प्रत्यगात्मानमिहावरुन्धे॥

"There is no other path to the attainment of Brahman, so auspicious for yogis, as devotion towards the Lord who is the Atma of all.

"With his mind full of wisdom, dispassion and devotion, he seeth Prakriti losing its power and Purusha as stainless.

"Where the good gather, there are heard the stories that give knowledge of My Power, and are as nectar to the ear and heart. Listening to them, he turneth rapidly to the path of Moksha with faith and joy and devotion.

"Turning away with dispassion from sensuous sights and sounds because of devotion to Me, he dwelleth ever in thought on (the mysteries of) My creation, and thus, restraining his mind, essayeth the straight paths of yoga and attaineth union.

"Giving up the service of the attributes of Prakriti, his knowledge and yoga (realisation of Unitv) blossoming with (the help of) vairagya, and his devotion offered unto Me, he realiseth Me as the Pratyagatma (the Inmost Self)."

स्वभावमे के कवयो वद्न्ति कालं तथान्वे परिमुह्यमानाः।
देवस्यैष महिमा तु लोकेयेनेंद भ्राम्यते ब्रह्मचक्रम्।

* * *

तमी श्वणणां परमं महे श्वरं तं देवताना परमं च दैवतम्।
पति पतीनां परमं परस्तात् विद्‌ाम देंव भुवनेशमीडयम्॥

न तस्य कार्य करणच्च विद्यते न तत्समश्चाभ्यधिकश्चहृश्ते।
परास्य शक्तिर्विंबिधैव श्रूयते स्वाभविकी ज्ञानवलक्रिया च॥
न तस्य कश्चित् पतिरक्ति नोके न चेशिता नैव च तस्य लिङ्कम्।
सकारणं करणधिपाधिपो न न चास्य कश्चिज्जनिता न चाधिपः॥
एको वशी निष्क्रियाणां बहूनामकं बीजं बहुधायः करोति।
तमात्मस्थंयेऽनुपश्यन्ति धीरास्तेषां सुखं शाश्वतं नेतरेषाम्॥
नित्यो नित्यानां चेतनश्चेतनाना-
मेको बहूनायो विदधाति कामान्।
तत्कारशं सांख्ययोगधिगम्यं
ज्ञात्वा देवं मुच्यते सर्वपाशैः॥

"From its own nature, some Sages say, others from time arising (came the universe); verily from the majesty of God revolves in this world the Brahma-wheel.

* * *

"Him of Ishvaras the supreme and great Ishvara, Him of Devas the supreme Divinity, of Lords the Lord, the greatest of the great, God, the adorable Ruler of the worlds, (Him) we know.

"He needeth no instrument nor hath aught to do, nor is there any found who is equal or superior to Him; His supreme energy is self-dependent and manifold, Wisdom, Power and Activity.

"None in the world is His lord, nor his ruler, nor His cause; He is the Cause, the Ruler of the rulers of the senses, of Him there is no source, no sovereign.

"The one Ruler of the many actionless, He maketh manifold the seed; therefore the wise who perceive Him within themselves, for them is eternal joy, for more others.

"Eternal of Eternals, Intelligence of Intelligences, One among many, who fulfilleth the wishes of all—having known that Cause, attained by the Sankhya and the Yoga, (man) is freed from all bonds.

भराजके हि लोकेऽस्मिन् सर्वतो विद्रते भयात्।
रक्षार्थमस्य सर्वस्य राजानमसृजत् प्रभुः।
इन्द्रानिलयमार्काणमग्नेश्च वरुणस्य च।
चन्द्रवित्तेशयोश्चैव मात्रा निर्हृत्य शाश्वतीः।।

* * *

तदर्थे सर्वभूतानां गोप्तारं धर्म्ममात्मजम्।
ब्रह्मातेजोमयं दएडमसृजत्पूर्वमीश्वरः।

* * *

दराडः शास्ति प्रजास्सर्वा दाड एवाभिरक्षति
दराडः सुप्तेषु जागर्ति दराडं धर्मं विदुर्बुधाः

* * *

तस्याहुः संप्रणतारं राजानं सत्यवादिनम्।
समीक्ष्श्कारिणां प्राज्ञं धर्मकामार्थकोविदम्।।
तं राजा प्रणयन्सम्यग्त्रिबर्गेणमिवर्धते।
कामात्मा विषमः क्षुद्रो दणडेनैव निहन्यते।।
दणडो हि समुहत्तेजो दुर्धरश्चाकृतात्मभिः।
धर्माद्विचलिंत हन्ति नृपमेव सबान्धवम्।।

"For the protection of the whole world God created the King, when the Kingless people were scattered through fear."

"(He created the King) out of immortal portions ktaen from Indra, Vayu, Yama, the Sun, the Fire, Varuna, the Moon and the Lord of wealth."

* * *

"For him the Lord created His own son Dharma, the Protector of all beings, as the Danda (Sceptre, or Rod of power) clothed with the Brahma-radiance."

* * *

"The Danda governeth all the people, the Danda alone protecteth; the Danda waketh while others sleep, the wise know the Danda as Dharma."

* * *

"They declare the wielder of Danda to be the King, that speaketh the truth, acteth after deliberation, is wise, and versedin Dharma, Kama and Artha.

"Wielding it righteously, the King increaseth in all three; but if he be given up to Kama, unjust and mean, then he himself is slain by the Danda.

"A great fire is the Danda, Difficult to be borne by those who have not achieved the Self; it slayeth, together with his family, the Kind that strayeth from Dharma"

तेन धर्मोत्तरश्चायं कृतो लोको महात्मना।
रष्जिताश्च प्रजाः सर्वास्तेन राजेति शब्द्यते॥

"By the grate-souled King was this wold made full of Dharma an all the People were gladdened; hence is he called the King."

राजा प्रजानां हृदयं गरीयो
गतिः प्रतिष्ठा सुखमुत्तमं च।
समाश्रिता लोकमिमं परं च
ज्यन्ति समयक्र पुरुषा नरेन्द्र॥
नराधिपश्चाप्यनुशिष्य मेदिनीं
दमेन सत्येन च सौदृदेन।
मद्विङ्किरिष्ठिा क्रतुभिर्महायशा-
स्त्रिविष्टपे स्थानमुपैति शाश्वतम्॥

"The King is the inmost heart of his people, he is their refuge, their honour, and their highest happiness; relying on Lem, they conquer righteously this world and the next.

"The King also, having governed the. earth with self-control, with truth, and with the heart of compassion, having sacrificed with many sacrifices, attaineth to fair fame and everlasting seat in Svarga."

उपाध्यायन्दशाचार्य श्राचार्यणं शतं पिता।
सहस्त्रं तु पितृन्माता गौरवेणतिरिच्यते।।

"Ten Upadhyayas doth the Acharya exceed and a hundred Acharyas the Father; but the Mother exceedeth even a thousand Fathers in the right to be honored."

आचार्यश्व पिता चैव माता भ्राता च पूर्वजः।
नार्तेनाप्यवमन्तव्या ब्राह्मणेन विशेषतः।।

* * *

तेषां त्रयाणां शुश्रूषा परमं तप उच्यते।

* * *

त एव हि त्रयो लोकास्त एव त्रय श्राश्रमाः।
त एव हि त्रयो वेदास्त एवोक्तास्त्रयोऽग्रयः।।

* * *

सर्वे तस्याहृता धर्मायस्यैते त्रय श्राद्दताः।
अनाहृतास्तुयस्यैते सर्वास्तस्याफलाः किया:।।

"The Teacher, the Father, the Mother, and an elder Brother must not be treated with disrespect, especially by a Brahmana, though one be grievously offended (by them).

"The service of these three is declared to be the best austerity.

* * *

"For they are declared to be the three worlds, the three orders, the three Vedas, they the three sacred fires.

* * *

"All duties have been fulfilled by him who honours these three; but to him who honours them not, all rites remain fruitless."

ऊर्ध्वं प्राणा ह्युत्क्रामन्तियूनः स्थविर आयति।
प्रत्युत्थनाभिवादाभ्यपां पुनस्तान्प्रतिपद्यते॥
अभिवादनशीलस्य नित्यं वृद्धोपसेविनः।
चत्वारि तस्य वर्धन्त आयुः प्रज्ञायशो बलम्।

"The vital airs of a young man mount upwards to leave his body when an elder approaches; but by rising to meet him and saluting, he recovers them.

"He, who habitually salutes and constantly pays reverence to the aged, obtains an increase of four things: length of life, knowledge, fame and strength.

CHAPTER 9

VIRTUES AND VICES IN RELATION TO EQUALS

We have next to consider our relations with the equals that surround us on every side, and to know what virtues should be developed, what vices avoided, in order to make our home and our outer relations harmonious and happy. Let us first think of those of the home, for they are of primary importance; pure and happy homes, in which family virtues are practised, make the foundation of prosperous States, of successful nations. We have seen the relations that should exist between parents and children, and we must now study those that should be found between husband and wife, between brothers and sisters.

The Hindu books are full of stories of the love that should bind a husband and wife together, or *Conjugal Love.* "Husband and wife are the same,"[178] says Manu; they are one, not two; love makes the two into one—love protective, sheltering, tender, on

178 Manusmriti, ix–45,

the side of the husband; love yielding, sweet, devoted, on the side of the wife. "Let mutual fidelity continue until death."[179] Rama- chandra and Sita form an ideal husband and wife; they enjoy all life's happinesses together, and suffer together all life's sorrows; they take counsel together in all perplexities, and share together all difficulties. We see them first in unclouded bliss, Prince and Princess, happy as the day is long; when the coronation of Ramachandra approaches, we see them fasting and praying together; when the shock of the sentence of exile comes, Sita accepts it carelessly at first caring only for her husband's presence, and she would go with him, she "whose heart is wholly thine, knowing not another, ever clinging to thee resolute to die if left by thee." Thorns would touch her skin like soft linen, dust would be as sandal-powder, grass would serve as blanket, roots and leaves as pleasant food, so long as she was by her husband's side. "O Rama, thy company is heaven, thy absence hell." Only when he pleads with her to remain behind, does her heart fail her. And when he bids her come she tosses gaily to her attendants all her costly robes and priceless jewels, stripping herself of all that women love, without a sigh, caring only for the joyous fact that exile could not separate husband and wife. Happy as a girl, she is said to be playing in the forest glades unmindful of the lost royal splendour, since she is, night and day, at Rama's side. But though so blithe, she yet is wise, and we hear her counselling her husband with grave thoughtful words, as they wander on the outskirts of the forest of Dandaka. When she is carried away by Ravana, the mighty Rakshasa, how her husband's love breaks forth in protracted search, in wild outbursts of lament. "Sita ! Sita !" he cries in his anguish as he searches for her, "art thou hiding, art thou playing? Oh come ! Such sport is my death." While laments and seeks, Sita is exposed to every temptation to be unfaithful, to every terror and cruel threat. "Devoted to one husband, I will never

179 Manusmriti, ix—101.

sin against him. With wealth and riches thou canst not tempt me. As the rays of the sun are his own, so am I Raghava's alone."[180]

And hear the story of Savitri, who won her husband from the grasp of Yama, King of Death. King Ashvapati, of the Madra lands, obtained a daughter by long worship of the Devas. They called her Savitri. Fair was she as a figure of gold, and sweet as the jessamine flower, and the people worshipped her as a Devi, come to them for their good deeds. When she came of age, her father said to her: "Choose thou a fitting husband for thyself." And she went forth asearch, with royal retinue. When she returned, after the lapse of many months, the Rishi Narada was staying with her father; and in his presence she announced the choice that she had made. "King Dyumatsena of the ShAlva country, old and blind and driven from his country by his enemies, lives in a forest, leading a hermit's life. His son, Satyavan, have I chosen for my spouse." Then Narada said: "Alas ! O King ! innocent Savitri hath done ill." "Is he not fitting mate for Savitri?" the King asked Narada. "Is he weak in mind or body, wanting in forgiveness or in courage?" Narada said: "In nothing is he wanting of all this. Strong and radiant as the sun himself is Satyavan, generous like Rantideva, just like Shibi, magnificent like Yayati, and beautiful like the moon. But all this wealth of virtues must pass away from the earth within a year. His span of life is very short." With sinking heart Savitri heard the Sage's words, yet said: "But once can a person say 'I *give away.*' And I have said it once: 'I give myself away to Satyavan.' I cannot choose again." Narada said: "Because thy daughter wavers not, O King ! I give my blessing to the marriage;" and went away.

Swift messengers went to Dyumatsena, and he sent back word to Ashvapati: "I once myself desired alliance with thee, but saw not how to ask for it in my fallen state. Now that the blessed Savitri is coming to me of her own accord, I know for sure that Lakshmi's self is coming back unto our ancient house." So the marriage came to pass. Joyously

180 Ramayana passim.

Savitri passed from her palaces to the hermit's cottage. Eagerly she attended to the least wants of her aged father-in-law and motherin-law, rejoicing to perform the humblest duties of the household, and by her tender ways and loving words enslaved the heart of her husband. But ever underneath all this, the fire of secret agony lighted by the words of Narada burned within her soul; and ever she counted the days of the prescribed year. At last the hour appointed for the death of Satvavan was only four days distant. Then she resolved to seek the help of the Devas by fast and prayer. And all the three days she fasted, taking not a drop of water. Early she rose on the morning of the fateful day, finished the morning rites, and touched the feet of her elders. All the ascetics dwelling in that forest blessed her on that day, saying that she should never know the pangs of widowhood. And when the time came for Satyavan to go forth with his axe upon his shoulder into the wood for work, as usual, she made her heart strong and followed him. He asked in wonder why; but she said she wished to go with him that day; and so they went, beholding the beauties of the hills, the waters, the woods, and the birds and beasts. Then Satyavan began his daily labours, filled his wallet with fruit and felled dried branches for fuel. But suddenly a faintness came upon him and his head ached greatly, and he said this to Savitri and lay down. Then Savitri placed his head on her lap and sat, with breaking heart, awaiting she knew not what. All at once she beheld a majestic and awe-striking form, dark yet shining, clad in red attire, standing beside her, and gazing with fixed yet flashing eyes at Satyavan. Gently she placed her husband's head on the ground, stood up and made obeisance. And the form said: "The days of Satyavan are ended: I am Yama, Lord of Death; and because he is so virtuous, I have come to take him away myself, rather than send my emissaries as usual." And he drew the Sukshma Sharira of Satyavan from his fleshy body, and departed with it towards the south. And Savitri also followed. Then Yama said: "Desist, O Savitri ! go back and perform the funeral rites of thy lord. Thou hast discharged thy duty, and come as far behind thy husband as mortal may go." Savitri replied: "Whither my husband goeth, thither I go. This is the eternal law for man and wife. If I have loved my lord with undivided love, if I have served my elders reverently, if there be any power in penances, then be my path unchecked, out of thy favour, Yama!" And innocently like a little child she repeated the lessons of dharma that her loving elders and her own gentle soul had taught her, "By faithful service, treading household ways, to wisdom have I won and to religious merit. Close not these ways, O Death, depriving me of my gathered fruits." "Wise and reasonable art thou, O Savitri, and thy words are sweet. Save thy husband's life, I give thee any boon." "His father lives in darkness, gracious King; by thy favour let his eyes once more behold the day." "Fairest of earth's daughters, I grant the boon thou seekest. And now return, O weary earth-born feet, that may not tread the gloomy path of Death." "Where he, my husband, goes, I still must follow. Fruitful is righteous company, O King of Death, and sweet is it to dwell with one like thee. Not fruitless may such fair abiding prove." "Take then a second boon as fruit, O peerless lady, but ask not for thy husband's soul," said Yama. "Give then, O King of mortal worlds, his kingdom to my husband's father, his kingdom rent from him by evil men." "He shall regain his throne," said Yama, "and reign thereon. And now go back, fair dame, nor follow further." But with sweet words and honeyed praises, Savitri still followed the Lord of Death, and won from him two other boons, one hundred sons for her father, and one hundred for herself. When the fourth boon was granted, Savitri spoke in praise of righteous living and of high discharge of duty, till Yama, charmed by her eloquence and wisdom, granted her yet another boon, and Savitri quickly claimed her husband's life, since Yama had granted her a hundred sons, and righteousness would be infringed if other were their father save her husband. Thus did a faithful wife win back from Death her husband, and brought to his family prosperity, riches, and length of days, since even Yama, King of Death, is weaker than a pure wife's faithful love.[181]

181 Mahabharatam. Vana Parva, ccxcii—ccxcviii.

Nor can the Hindu boy forget the story of Damayanti, the wife of Nala. Nala, son of Virasena, and King of the Nishadhas, loved Damayanti, daughter of Bhima, the King of the Vidarbhas, and Damayanti loved Nala, though they had not met each other, but each had only heard the other's praises as being incomparable upon earth. Now the Svayamvara of the princess was proclaimed, and thereto went King Nala, and Damayanti chose him to be her husband, although the Devas, Indra, Agni, Varuna and Yama, were among the suitors for her hand; and Nala and Damayanti lived together in great love for eleven happy years, and two children were born to them. In the twelfth year came Pushkara, and challanged King Nala to play him at dice, and Nala played, and lost again and again, till at length he had lost to Pushkara his kingdom and all his wealth, even his garments, and went forth an exile, with only one cloth, half covering his body. Then Damayanti, his wife—having sent her children to her father's care when she saw how the games were going—went forth after him, clad also in a single cloth, and in the outskrits of the city they wandered, hungry and athirst. To complete their misery, Nala lost his cloth in the attempt to catch therewith some birds for food, and hopeless and desperate, he wished Damayanti to be spared the suffering of hunger, and repeatedly pointed out to her the road to her former home. But Damayanti, clung to him, weeping, sobbing that she would not leave him, that when he was weary she would soothe him, for in every sorrow there was no such medicine as a loving and faithful wife. Presently, wearied out, she lay sleeping on the bare ground, and Nala argued with himself that it would be kinder to leave her, so that she might seek her relatives, than to keep her wandering in misery with him. Thus thinking, he cut in half, with a sword that was lying near, the cloth she wore, leaving one half around her; and wrapping round himself the other half, he fled from her, mad with grief. The hopeless Damayanti awaking, found herself alone, and bitter was her grief, more for Nala's loneliness than for her own loss. She sought her husband eagerly, but found him not—

found instead a huge serpent, that wrapped her closely in his coils. How she escaped, and what fresh perils befell her ere she found at last shelter as companion to a princess of the Chedis, is told at length in the *Nalopakhyana,* Meanwhile Nala had rescued a snake ringed round with fire, and by the magic of the snake his form was changed and became unrecognisable, and he wandered till he reached the city of King Rituparna, whose charioteer he became. Thus were husband and wife severed, they who loved each other so dearly and so well. Now King Bhima sent forth Brahmanas to search for his daughter and for Nala, and one of them, Sudeva by name, recognised the sad Queen as she sat in the King of Ghedis' palace, and told her piteous story to the Queen-mother, who proved to be her mother's sister. Then Damayanti, in spite of warmest offers of hospitality, departed to her father's house, and King Bhima sent out again messengers to seek Nala, charged to bear a message to be uttered loudly in every gathering of men, which in veiled allusions, intelligible to Nala only, prayed him to return to his loving, sorrowing wife. Long they sought, and at last found one who, after hearing the outcried message, spoke sadly of wives whom their husbands had deserted, and he was called Bahuka, charioteer of Rituparna, King in Ayodhya. Returning to Damayanti Parnada, the messenger, told what had been said, and her quick woman's wit devised a way by which to bring Nala to her side. "Go to King Rituparna," she said, "and tell him that Damayanti holds another Svayamvara on the morrow after thy arrival in Ayodhya." For she knew that none save Nala could so drive as to reach her father's palace from Ayodhya, within so brief a space. As she planned, so it happened, Rituparna bade Bahuka drive him swiftly to the city of the Vidarbhas, and Bahuka, sore at heart, chose swift steeds and drove them, as only he could drive, reaching the city of the Vidarbhas by that same evening, and there, by Damayanti's tender wiles, he was led to give signs that he was indeed Nala, as she suspected, for he wept over his children when he saw them, and he cooked as only Nala could cook; then she bade them bring Bahuka into her presence, and husband and true wife recognised each other, and long thereafter lived they in wedded bliss, their kingdom regained, and their children around them.[182]

Moreover, a wife who truly loves and serves her husband gains more of inner development and knowledge than she can gain by long austerities and painful penances. For thus we read in the story of the Brahmana's wife who angered Kaushika. Now the Brahmana Kaushika made great tapas. One day he sat in meditation under a tree, when a crane sitting on a branch befouled his person. He opened his eyes and looked up angrily at the crane; and, such was the psychic power stored in Kaushika by his tapas, that the crane was killed by that angry glance as if struck by lightning. Kaushika was sad at the death of the crane, and glad also with the pride of tested power. He went into the neighbouring town to beg as usual for his daily meal, and asked the first good housewife that he came across for it. As she was fetching him some food her husband came in, tired with his daily work, covered with dust. Asking Kaushika to stay a while, she began to attend to her husband. Some time elapsed and Kaushika's impatience grew. When she came back to him at last with the food he needed, he looked at her with angrier eyes than he had looked with at the crane, and asked her how she had neglected the Brahmana for so long. She answered gently: "My duty to my husband is more urgent than to thee. Restrain thy wrath and learn forgiveness, Brahmana ! Look not at me with anger; that will injure thee. I am no crane !" Kaushika was thunderstruck and questioned her and she replied: "No penances have I performed to gather psychic powers; only served my husband single-mindedly. If thou wouldst learn yet more about the virtues of our simple household duties, go to the fowler of distant Mithila." Kaushika went, with a humbled mind, to Mithila, and stood at the fringe of the great crowd of customers around the fowler's shop. The fowler saw Kaushika, went up to him, and, bowing low to the Brahmana,

182 Mahabharatam, Vana Parva, liii—Ixxix,

said: "I know why the faithful housewife sent thee to me, and shall resolve thy doubts and show thee why I can do so." Then the fowler took Kaushika to his home, and shewed him his aged parents, as we have already seen.[183]

How brothers should show *Brotherly Love* we read in the whole story of the *Ramayana,* and it is said that Lakshmana was like Rama's life, so dear and close the bond, nor would they sleep apart, nor apart engage in sport; we see him follow Ramachandra into the forest, and stand waking on watch while Rama slept; we see him sharing in the search for Sita, ever wise in counsel and loving in sympathy; and when Lakshmana lies senseless, arrow-pierced, before Lanka, hear Rama's piteous cry: "What have 1 to do with life and what with war, now Lakshmana lies wounded on the field of battle? Why, forsaking me dost thou wander in other worlds? Without thee, life and victory, nay, Site's self, are worthless."

The whole story of the *Mahabharatam* shows how brotherly love and union lead to prosperity and fame; for never do we find the Pandavas with warring interests, or leading separated lives. Yudhishthira represents the family, and all the efforts of the younger are directed to his enrichment and his prosperity. For him they fight, and all the wealth they gain is gained for him; for him Arjuna seeks and wins the divine weapons, by sharp tapas and fierce, struggles and long and weary wanderings. And equally does Yudhishthira cherish them, regarding their joys and sorrows as his own.

Yudhishthira has risen into Svarga, and looks round on every side to find his brothers and his wife. "I desire to go whither my brothers are gone," he cries again and again, and nowhere, among radiant Devas and triumphant Rajas, can he see the faces he so dearly loves. "Ye mighty ones!" at last he cries, "what is your heaven to me apart from them? That is heaven where my brothers are. This is not heaven for me." Then the Pevas bade a heavenly messenger lead forth the King, and take him to the land where now his loved ones lived; and

183 Mahabharatam, Vana Parva, ccv.

turning their backs on Svarga they went out, and began to tread a path that led into ever-deepening gloom. Darkey and darker grew the air, gloomier and gloomier yet the shadowy way. Foul things of nauseous smell and horrid shape crowded round them as they went, and beneath their feet the ground was slippery with blood, and was strewn with fragments of the corpses of the slain. Sharp thorns and piercing leaves obstructed it, and burning sand, and iron stones white-hot. Astounded, the King questioned his celestial guide, who told him that he had been bidden to lead him thither, but if he were weary, he could return. Slowly, doubtfully, Yudhishthira turned, sure that his brothers .could hot dwell in region so foul and evil but as he turned sad cries arose on every hand, and piteous prayers that he would stay a while. "Who are you?" asked the wondering King, and answers sobbed from every side. "I am Karna." "I am Bhishma." "I am Arjuna." "I am Nakula." "I am Sahadeva." "I am Draupadi." And so with others, dearly loved on earth. "Go back, go back to Svarga," cried the King, wrought to anger by his brothers' wrongs; "go back to those who sent you here as guide. Not with them my place, but here, here, where my loved ones dwell. Go thou back to Svarga's barren joys; better with these in pain than there in lonely bliss." And as he spake heaven's fragrance breathed around, and all was balmy air and shining light and thronging Devas For stronger than hell is love, and fidelity than pain.

Among the virtues to be shown outside the family, *Hospitality* stands in the first rank, and how highly it is to be valued may be seen in the story of the half-golden mongoose that attended the great sacrifice of King Yudhishthira, where all the arches and the stakes and sacrificial vessels were of gold, and whereat all men took as they would of gems and money, none forbidding them. Yet cried the mongoose, that the sacrifice of the wealth there gathered was of less worth than a small measure of powdered barley, given by a poor Brahmana to his guest. And thus he told the tale. There was a Brahamana who kept the unchha vow, and daily lived on the grains of corn he gathered, making one frugal meal a day, he and his wife, with son and daughter-in-law. And a terrible famine laid waste the land and few were the grains left upon the husking-ground by threshers, and ever thinner and thinner grew he and his family, till they were but as living skeletons. One day it happened that he had gathered a little barley, and, having powdered it, the wife divided it into four, that each might have a scanty meal and joyfully they sat down to eat. But ere yet they had touched the little heaps of grain, a guest stood in the doorway, and quickly rising, the Brahmana brought him in, and gave him water and a seat, and then set before him his own share of the scanty food. The guest ate, but still was hungry, and the wife brought her share and placed it in her husband's hands that he might put it before the guest. "Shaking art thou with weakness, mother of my son," he said: "keep thou the food and eat, lest my home lose its sunshine." But she pressed on him the food, that the dharma of hospitality might not be broken, and, with a sigh, he took and gave. Yet still the guest was fain for more, and the son brought his meagre share, and the brahmana, aching for his son's hunger and the emaciation of his youthfull body, laid that third portion before the guest. But, alas ! even then the guest was still hungry, for each little share was as nothing for a hungry man, and the young wife's share was now held out to the host's shaking hands, but he drew them back with anguish at his heart. "Not yours, my little one, not yours, not yours." "Father of my son's father, " she said, with sweet humility of voice and gesture, "shut me not out from sharing your good deeds. As a Deva is a guest. Feed him, then, from this my food, which is as thine own flesh. " Weeping he took, and then with gentle smile laid it before his guest, who took and ate. Then, as the guest rose up, bright light shone out, and in the midst he stood, radiant and splendid; for truly was the guest a Deva, the Lord of Righteousness, Dharma, the strong and pure. And in a few grains that he had left uneaten, the mongoose rolled, and half his body turned to gold by the magic of that sacrifice, so priceless is the gracious virtue of hospitality, so transforming is its power.[184]

184 *Mahabharatam*, Vana Parva, iv—vi.

A wicked fowler, black in skin like his own deeds of daily murder of innocent brids and beasts, and red in the eyes like his burning malice against his victims, was once overtaken by a terrible thunderstorm, in the middle of a forest. The open glades were converted into lakes and the pathways into running streams in a moment. The higher lands to which he tried to find a way were invaded by bears and lions and other fierce denizens of the jungle. Shivering with cold, shaking with fear, he yet refrained not from his cruel habits.

Espying a poor she-pigeon lying on the ground, beaten down by the torrents of the rains and frozen with the cold he picked her up and mercilessly thrust her into the cage he carried. Wandering on he shortly came to a lordly tree that stood in the midst of the forest, and extended a benevolent shade and shelter to myriads of the feathered tribe. It seemed to have been placed there on purpose by the Creator for the good of all creatures, like a good man for the benefit of the world. The fowler took refuge beneath the. spreading boughs of the tree. By and by, the clouds dispersed, and the stars shone out. But the fowler was too far away from his home and resolved to pass the night under the tree. As he lay under the tree he heard the he-pigeon lamenting: "Alas! thou hast not yet returned, dear wife! What can have happened to thee? If that dear wife of mine, with her bright rose-eyes, sweet coo, and softest plumes, cometh not back to my nest, my life shall no longer be worth living. The house is not the home, in truth; the wife is the home. She eats when I eat, she bathes when I bathe; she rejoices when I rejoice, and sorrows when I sorrow. Yet if I am angry, she always speaks with sweetness only. Life is empty without such a spouse. Without such, a palace is an empty wilderness. Such a one is a trusted companion and beloved associatein all one's acts of virtue, profit and pleasure. The wife is the richest possession of her lord. She is his one unfailing associate in all the concerns of life. She is the best of medicines for all the diseases of the mind. There is no friend like unto the wife, no refuge better than she. "

Hearing the lament of her husband, the she- pigeon caged by the cruel fowler said to herself: "Unlimited is my happiness even in the midst of agony that my husband thinketh thus of me. She is no wife with whom her lord is not content. But we must also think of this poor fowler, overtaken by the cruel storm and kept away from home. He is now our guest, having taken shelter underneath our abode." And she cried aloud to her husband, explaining the plight of the fowler. The pigeon too, with instant sympathy, forgetting . his own sorrows, addressed the fowler: "Welcome to my house as honoured guest, and tell me what to do." The fowler said: "I am stiff with cold; warm me if thou canst." The bird gathered togather a heap of dead and fallen leaves; picked up one in his beak, flew and very soon returned with a tiny ember on it from some neighbouring village. In a moment the fowler found himself warmed by a grateful fire, and the bird asked him again for service to be done. The fowler asked for food this time. The bird thought: "I have no stores wherewith to feed him; and yet a hungry guest may not be left unfed. " As he reflected deeply, a new light arose within his mind and he cried to his guest: "I shall gratify thee ! I have heard in former days from high-souled Rishis, and the Devas and Pitris also that there is great merit in honoring a guest. O friend ! do thou be kind to me and accept my humble service !" With this he flew around the fire three times and then entered the flames, offereing his body to his guest for food.

At that awful act of uttermost guest-honouring, an unknown horror of his own past life on sin seized on the mind of the fowler, tearing up his evil nature by its deepest roots, and leaving him all shattered. "Thou art my highest teacher, high-souled bird ! Thou showest me my duty ! From this day I expiate my sins, denying rosy comfort to this sin-fed body, evaporating it with all its crimes by daily fast and tapas, as the strong rays of the summer sun dry up a small and dirty pool. Taught by this example I shall practise righteousness alone henceforth." He threw away his club, his nets and traps and iron cage, and set at liberty the widowed mate of the deceased bird. The she-pigeon thus released, circled round the funeral pyre, of her husband, weeping: "Limited are the gifts that the woman receiveth from her father or her mother or her son. But the gifts that the husband giveth to her are limitless! He giveth her his all and all himself I After all these years of happiness with thee, I cannot live alone !" and she threw herself also into the fire.

With a new-born vision the fowler beheld the two ascending to heaven in glorious forms; and the more confirmed in his resolve thereby, he took up his abode in the forest, living a blameless life thenceforward, till the forest-fires, kindled by dried branches rubbing against each other in a summer-storm, consumed his body, as the penance had consumed his sins.

Readiness to forgive wrongs is a sign of a truly noble nature. It is. said of Ramachandra that a hundred injuries left no trace upon his memory, while one benefit was graven there. And listen how Vidura forgot insult and forgave. Kind Dhritarashtra craved Vidura's help touching the evil conduct of Duryodhana, and Vidura counselled his brother wisely but firmly, praying him to enforce on Duryodhana his duty of peace with his Pandava cousins, and to make his supporters win forgiveness from the wronged and exiled princes. At this, Dhritarashtra became much incensed, and hotly blamed his righteous brother, accusing him of partiality, and finally of foul disloyalty, adding gross insult to the charge and going from his brother's side in wrath. Then Vidura sadly sought the Pandavas, and told how he was sent away with angry words, and counselled them with wisdom, urging urbanity and gentle ways. And after Vidura had gone, King Dhritarashtra repented him of his harshness and injustice, and sent after him to beg him to return, exclaiming: "Go, O Sanjaya, and see if my brother lives, he whom I have driven away in angry madness. Never has he wronged me, nor committed any fault, while I have grievously wronged him. Seek him and bring him hither, Sanjaya, the wise." So Sanjay a went, wondering whether Vidura, the calm and strong, would pardon his weaker brother's changing moods, and become again the pillar of his throne. And going to the forest, he found Vidura, highly honoured by the princes and by all, and approaching him, prayed him to return. Then Vidura, without hesitating even for a moment, rose and took leave of his royal nephews, and hastened to his elder brother's presence, who prayed forgiveness for the wrong committed. Gently Vidura spoke: "O King, I have forgiven. Worthy of highest reverence art thou, my elder, my superior. Eagerly have I come, longing to see thy face. And if I seemed to favour the sons of Pandu, it was because a man's heart yearneth over those who are distressed, more from emotion than from reason. Dear are thy sons to me as they, O King, but the sorrows of the latter moved my heart." Thus gently and magnanimously spoke the younger brother, forgetting, as unimportant, the insults he had received.

Urbanity is a virtue very characteristic of the old Hindu life. We see the most exquisite politeness in language and in action, as we read how the great ones of the epic poems, good and bad alike, behaved towards guests and friends and foes. Ramachandra is gentle in speech, and prefaces his speeches with a kindly smile. Lakshmi the, Devi of Prosperity, speaking of the Danavas endued with sweet speech, with friendliness and with forgiveness, declares that She dwelt with them because of their virtues. When they gave way to wrath, and harshness, and unfair dealings, She left them, attended by the Devis who abide with Her— Hope, Faith, Intelligence, Contentment, Victory, Advancement and Forgiveness. So Narada is said to be sweet-speeched, large-hearted, straightforward, free from wrath and greed, and therefore everywhere regarded with respect and love. Again, Bhishma teaches that we should not disparage others by look, word or thought nor speak evil of any; that we should never injure any, nor behave with unfriendliness; that we should pass- with indifference opprobrious speeches, and, even- when another seeks to anger us, should still speak agreeably, and when slandered, we should not slander in return. So again Narada described a Naga, named Padma, who was walking on the- threefold path of acts, knowledge and devotion, and spoke of him as ever hospitable, practising forgiveness, and abstaining from inflicting injuries. He was truthful in word and free from malice, kind of speech and seeking the benefit of all. A Brahmana went to see him. and to learn from him, but on arriving at his house found him absent. His wife hospitably welcomed the stranger, and after exchanging courteous speech with her, he left her and waited patiently on the banks of the river the return of her husband. While waiting there, he did not eat, and the relatives of the absent. Naga, approaching him in great trouble of mind, urged that they were bound to show him hospitality. "The whole community, young and old, is being afflicted, since this thy fast implies that we are negligently leaving unperformed the duties of hospitality." Gently replied the Brahmana that by their kindly wishes they had fed him, but he could not eat until the Naga chief returned. Presently he arrived and in his conversation with his wife, we see the duties of the householder; his religion is in doing good to all; all who come as guests must be hospitably entertained; the householder must be gentle, free from wrath and arrogance, must be generous and truthful.[185] Thus of old was taught the duty of the citizen to those around him.

पितृभिर्भ्रातृभिश्चैताः पतिभिदर्वैरैस्तथा।
पूज्याभूषयितव्याश्च बहु कल्श्सधसमरप्युभिः॥
यत्रनार्यस्तु पूज्यन्ते रमन्ते तत्र देवताः।
यत्रैतास्तु न पूज्यन्ते सर्वास्तत्रफलाः क्रियाः॥
शोचन्ति जामयोयत्र विनश्यतशु तत्कुलम्।

185 Mahabharatam, Shiloti Parva, ccclvi—cc clxi.

न शोचन्ति तुयत्रैता वर्धते तद्धि सर्वदा॥
जामयोयानि गेहानि शपन्तसप्रतिपूजिताः।
तानि कृतयाहतानीव विनश्यन्ति समन्ततः॥[186]

"Women must be honoured and adorned by their fathers, brothers, husbands and brothers-in- law, who desire welfare.

"Where women are honoured, there the Devas are pleased; but where they are not honoured, no sacred rite is fruitful.

"Where the female relatives live in grief, the family soon perishes utterly; but that family in which they are not unhappy prospers ever.

"The houses in which female relatives, not being duly honoured, pronounce a curse, perish completely, as if destroyed by magic."

एतावानेव पुरुषोयज्जायात्मा प्रजेति ह।
विप्राः प्राहुस्तथा चैतद्या भर्ता सा स्मृताङ्गना॥[187]

"This is the extent of the man: his wife, himself and his children; Brahmanas thus declare that the husband and wife are known as the same."

श्रन्योन्यस्यसव्यभीचारो भवेदामराणान्तिकः।
एष धर्मःयमसयेप ज्ञेयःस्त्रीपुंसयोः परः॥
तथा नित्यंयतेयातां स्त्रीपुंसौ तु कृतक्रियौ।
यथा नातिचरेतां तो वियुत्त्कावितरेतरम्।[188]

"Let mutual fidelity continue until death; this may be considered as the summary of the highest law for husband and wife.

186 *Manusmriti*, iii, 55–58.

187 *Manusmriti*, ix–45.

188 *Ibid*, 101–102.

"Let man and woman, united in marriage, constantly exert themselves, that they be not disunited nor violate their mutual fidelity."

तृणानि भूमिरुदकं वाक् चतुर्थी च सूनृता।
एतान्यपि सतां गेहे नोच्छिद्यन्ते कदाचन॥
* * *
श्रप्रणोद्यीऽतिथिः सायं सूर्योढो गृहमेधिना।
काले प्राप्तस्त्वकाले वा नास्यानश्नन्गृहे वसेत्॥
न वै स्वयं तदश्नीयादतिथियन्न भोजयेत्।
घन्यंयशस्यमायुष्यं स्वर्ग्यं चातिथिभोजनम्॥[189]

"Grass, room, water and fourthly, a kind word; these are never wanting in the households of the good.

* * *

"A guest who is sent by the sun in the evening must not be driven away by a householder; whether he have come at a convenient or incon venient time, he must not stay in the house without entertainment.

"Let him (the householder) not eat any food which he does not offer to his guest; the hospitable reception of guests procures wealth, fame, long life, and heavenly bliss."

सत्यं ब्रूयात्प्रिंय ब्रूयान्नब्रूयात्सत्समप्रियम्।
प्रियं च नानृतं ब्रूयादेष धर्मः सनातनः॥[190]

"Let him speak the true, let him speak the pleasing, let him not speak an unpleasing truth, nor speak a pleasing falsehood this is the ancient law."

---

189 *Ibid*, iii, 101, 105—106.
190 *Manuismriti*, iv—138.

यस्त वाङ्मनसी शुद्धे सम्यग्गुप्तेङ च सर्वदा।
स वै सर्वमावाप्रोति वेदान्तोपगतं फलम्।
नारुन्तुदः स्यादार्तोऽपि न परद्रोहकर्मधीः।
ययास्योद्विजते वाचा नालोक्यां तामुदरियेत्।।[191]

"He whose speech and mind are pure and ever carefully guarded, he obtains all the fruit that is obtained by means of the Vedanta.

"Let him not, even though distressed, cut another to the quick (by his speech); nor meditate acts of hostility to others; let him never utter the malignant word that disturbs (the mind of the hearer)."

नास्तिक्यं वेदनिन्दां च देवतानां च कुत्सनम्।
द्वेषं स्तम्भं च मानं च क्रोधं तैक्षरायं च वर्जयेत्।।

"Let him avoid unbelief, censure of the Vedas and slighting of the Devas, hatred, obstinacy, pride, anger and harshness."

नारुन्तुदः स्यानू न नृशंसवादी
न हीनतः परम श्याददीत।
ययाऽस्य वाचा पर उद्विजेत
न तां वदे दुषतीं पापलोक्यां।।
अरुन्तुद परुषं तीक्षणवाचं
वाकंब कैर्वितुदन्तं मनुष्यान्।
विद्यादलक्ष्मीकतंम जनानां
मुख निबद्धां निऋर्ति वहन्तां।
वाक्सासका वदनान्निष्पतन्ति
यैराहतः शोचति रात्र्यहानि।
परस्य नामर्मसु ते पतन्ति
तान्पएिडतो नाबसृजेत्परेषु।।

191 *Manusmriti*, ii 160—162.

नहीहशं संवनन त्रिषु लोकेषु विद्यते।
दया मैत्री च भूंतषु दानं व मधुरा च वाक्॥
तस्मात्सांत्वं सदा वाच्यं न वाच्यं परुषं कचित्।
पुज्यान्संपूजयेद्द्यान्नय बाचेत् कदाचन॥

"Let no one utter cruel words, or wound (with them) the vitals (of another); let none seek to subdue his enemy by unfair means. Let him not utter that inauspicious speech, belonging to the evil worlds, whereby another is agitated.

"The man that ever wounds the vitals of others, harsh, and sharp of speech, ever piercing other men with the thorns of evil words, he is the man most abandoned of (Lakshmi) fortune, and ever beareth, bound to his mouth, an evil demon.

"They are verily arrows, these evil words that issue from the mouth; he who is wounded by them sorroweth night and day, for they wound the vitals. The wise man unlooseth not such (shafts) at others.

"There are no riches in the three worlds like unto these—compassion, friendliness to all beings, charity and sweet speech.

"Therefore ever speak gently and never harshly; honour the worthy; give, but ask not."

क्रुब्द्धः पापं नरः कुर्यात् क्रुब्द्धो हन्याद्गरूनति।
क्रुब्द्धः परुषया वाचाश्रेयसोऽव्यवमन्यते॥
श्रात्मानमपित च क्रुब्द्धः प्रेषयेद्यमसादनं।
एठान्दोषान्द्रपश्यङ्क्गिर्जितः क्रोधो मनीषिभिः॥

"The man that has given way to anger may commit any sip, he may slay even his elders, or insult those worthy of his reverence with harsh speech:

"He may send himself to the abode of Death Beholding these great faults in anger, have the wise ones conquered it."

किंस्विदेकपदं ब्रह्मन् पुरुषः समयगाचरन्।
प्रमाणं सर्वभूतानांयशश्चैवाप्नुयान्महत्॥
सांत्वमेकपदं श्रक पुरुषः सम्यगाचरत्।
प्रमाणं सर्वभूतानां यशश्चैवाप्नुयान्महत्॥
एतदेकपदं शक्र सर्वलोकसुखावहं।
आचरन्सर्वभूतेषु प्रियो भवति सर्वदा॥

"What *one* thing, O Brahmana (Indra asks of his Preceptor Brihaspati), if a man shall practise well, shall he become a standard for all beings, and attain to fame widespread?

"Gentleness is the *one* thing, O Shakra, which if a man will practise unremittingly, he shall become a standard for all beings and attain to fame widespread.

"This one thing bringeth joy to all the worlds; practising it towards all beings, the man becometh dear unto all and always."

यस्तु क्रोधं समुत्पन्नं प्रज्ञया प्रतिबाधते।
तेजस्विनं तं विद्वांसो मन्यंते तत्त्वदर्शिनः॥

"He that with wisdom suppresseth the anger that hath risen within him, him the learned knowers of truth declare to be the true

CHAPTER 10

VIRTUES AND VICES IN RELATION TO INFERIORS

As we go more and more into the world, we come across many people who are much younger than ourselves, people of the next or of later generations, people also who are less -educated, or who are poorer, or below us in social rank. with such people, inferior to ourselves in some special point or generally, we enter into relations, and we need to know what virtues we should cultivate, what vices we should avoid, if our relations with them are to be harmonious.

The first and most Obvious of these relations is that with our youngers, and the best examples of the necessary virtues are seen in the relations of parents to their children. *Tenderness, Compassion, Gentleness, Kindness,* how strongly these virtues shine out in loving parents, and how happy they make the home. Father and mothers love their children, suffer in their sufferings, are glad in their pleasures, feel sympathy with them in everything.

This fact is beautifully brought out in an ancient story, the story of the sorrow of Surabhi when her children suffer. In days of yore, Surabhi, the celestial mother of the race of cows and bulls, once stood before the King of the Devas, shedding tears. Indra asked her eagerly: "Why dost thou weep, auspicious mother of the cows? Hath any ill befallen thee?" Surabhi replied: "No evil hath befallen this body of mine; but I am grieving for my offspring. See, O King of the worlds, that cruel husbandman beating my feeble son that labours at the plough, and falls again and again in his weakness. The stronger of the pair beareth his burthen easily; but the weaker beareth it with difficulty. It is for him I grieve with heavy heart and tearful eyes." Indra asked in wonder: "But thousands of thy offspring are thus treated every day I" And Surabhi replied: "And for each of those thousands that suffers thus, I weep, O King, and I weep more for the one that is weaker than for the others." Then Indra understood the love there is in the mother's heart for her child in suffering, and poured down showers on the fields of earth, and sent comfort to man and beast alike.[192]

Very tenderly is shown the love of Dasharatha for Ramachandra, his perfect son, both in his joy over his splendid qualities and his

192 Ramayana, Ayodhyakandam.—Ixiy.

sorrow in his exile. Listen to his words, as he addresses his princes and his nobles, when he proposes to instal his son as his successor, to seat him on the throne. Every sentence breathes his love and pride. And when Kaikeyi has claimed her boons, and demands Rama's exile to the forest, see Dasharatha falling at her feet, declaring that though the world might live without the sun, without Rama he could not live: "I lay my head at thy feet. Be merciful to me. Have pity on me, aged and on the verge of death." Arid so true was this, that when Shri Rama at last tore himself away from his father, that father went home broken-hearted, and died from grief for his exiled son. And remember the pitiful scene between Ramachandra and his mother Kaushalya when he carries her the news of his exile. He shall not go, she cries in her anguish; without him she will pine away and die. Or, if he be fixed in will to go, in loving obedience to his father's orders, then will she also tread the forest paths. "Like unto a cow following its young one, shall I follow thee, O my darling, wheresoever thou shalt go."[193]

And see the woe of Kuriti, when her five noble sons, the Paindavas, are driven away into exile after the shameful gambling match in which all was lost. Kunti—bravest of women and of mothers, who, when the hour of battle came, bade Shri Krishna tell her sons that the time had come for them for which a Kshattriya woman bore a son, and that even life should be laid down for honour's sake—this Kunti wailed, broken-hearted, and could scarce force herself away from her sons, could scarce forbear to follow them as they went forth.

Or again, note the agony of Arjuna over the death of his heroic son, Abhimanyu; as he returns to the camp from the field of battle, he feels unaccustomed cloud enwrap him and turns to Shri Krishna for help, for explanation. Eagerly he questions his brothers, who fear to answer him, and with sad heart feels the piercing anguish of his son's death; and surely the youth must have thought, as his

193 Ramayana, xx—xxv.

foes closed in around him, "My father will rescue me from this fierce storm, but his father came not to his helping, and he fell, pierced by a hundred wounds. Not to have been present to protect his child—that was the thought that stung Arjuna to madness, for ever the heroic soul longs to protect the weaker; much more then when the hero is a father, and the weaker is a well-loved son.

This duty of *Protecting the Weak* is incarnated in the righteous King, and it is the fulfilment of this duty which awakens the loyalty of his subjects.

"To protect his subjects is the cream of kingly duties,"[194] says Bhishma. "The King should always bear himself towards his subject as a mother towards the child of her wombas the mother, disregarding those objects that are most cherished by her, seeks the good of her child alone, even so, without doubt, should Kings conduct themselves."[195] So stringent is this duty of protection, that King Sagara exiled his own eldest son, Asamanjas, because that prince, in reckless cruelty, drowned the children of his subjects in the river.[196]

Many are the stories of the ways in which good Kings defended the weak who trusted in their protection, and this sense of duty embraced the lower animals as well as man. A dog had followed King Yudhisthira the just from Hastinapura, through all his weary wanderings on the last great journey, and had crossed with him the vast desert, the only surviyor of that long travel save the King himself. Indra has come down from heaven to fetch the kings to Svarga, and bids him mount the car and speed upwards with him. The King stoops, and gently touches the head of his faithful canine follower: "This dog, O Lord of the Past and of the Present, is very devoted to me. He too should go. My heart is full of compassion for this poor child of earth." "No dog may tread

194 *lbid,* Shanti Parva—Iviii.

195 *Mahabharatam,* Shanti Parya, Ivi.

196 *Ibid,* Ivii.

the heavenly fields," said Indra in reply. "Immortality and a state like unto my own, O King, far-stretching fortune, high success and all the joys of heaven—these thou hast won to-day. Cast off then the dog, who hinders thine ascent. Naught cruel is there in the act; earthbound, he dwells on earth." "O thou of a thousand eyes, O thou of righteous living, an Aryan may not commit an act unworthy of an Aryan. I care not for a bliss bought by the casting off of one who is to me devoted." "Heaven has no place for persons followed by dogs," said Indra sternly'. "Abandon the dog, and come. Time passes swiftly." "To abandon the devoted is a sin, sin immeasurable, say the wise. As black as the slaying of a Brahmana is this sin of abandoning the week. O Indra, mighty one, not for the sake of winning happiness will I cast away this dog." In vain does Indra command or plead; the King remains unmoved. Nor can sophistry confuse his clear vision: he had abandoned his brothers and his wife, why not his dog? says Indra. "This is well known in all the worlds that with the dead is neither friendship nor yet quarrel. When my brothers and Krishna fell and died, no power was mine to bring them back to life; hence I abandoned them. I did not abandon them so long as they were living. This one lives. To terrorise the seeker for protection, to slay a woman, to steal what belongeth to a Brahmana, to injure a friend, to each of these crimes, methinks, is equal the sin of abandoning one so devoted." And then the dog vanished and Dharma, Deva of righteousness, stood in celestial glory where had crouched the dog, and with him and Indra, hymned by Devas, praised by Sages, the righteous King was carried to the heavenly world.[197]

Hear yet another tale of ancient days.

King Shibi, son of Ushinara, sat in his spacious hall, in the midst of his assembled court. All at once, a dove flew in, and, rushing through the air, flung itself into the broad lap of the King, panting breathless, fainting with fatigue and fear. As the

---

197 *Mahabharatam*, Mahaprasthiinika Parva,—iii.

King stroked and smoothed its ruffled feathers in a wondering tenderness, soothing back its breath and life with his caresses, an angry hawk dashed into the hall also, and came to a sudden pause before the King. In reviving terror, the dove cried out in a human voice: "Thou art the sovereign of this land wherein I dwell. I have a right to thy protection too. I come to thee for refuge from my enemy." But the hawk said also with the human voice: "I too reside within thy sovereignty, O King, and this is my appointed food by Providence itself. If thou deniest it to me, then surely thou refusest me my right." The King pondered a while and said: "Ye both are right ! Thou hast a right, O dove, that I protect thy innocent life from harm; and thou, O hawk, that I deprive thee not of thy just food ! But thus shall I resolve this knot of dharma. Take thou other food from me, O hawk, till thou art full! " But the hawk said: "I must have the dove itself, none other; or if other, then flesh from thine own body, O King, of the weight of this very dove." The angry ministers would have slain at once the hawk that menaced thus the priceless life of their beloved master, and cried out against the petty thing. But King Shibi said: "I sit here as the sovereign, not for small or great, not for dove or hawk, but as living embodiment of Dharma, as example to my people. If I fail in the. small, I shall fail in the great also; and my people shall fail grievously, imitating me. Bring up a pair of scales !" Stricken with a great sorrow, powerless to disobey, setting their teeth against the outwelling groans, the ministers brought up scales. With one gentle hand, the King placed the dove into one, and with the other strong hand he hewed a piece of flesh from His own limbs. But the dove was too heavy. And the King hewed off another piece and the dove was much too heavy still. And the wondering King hewed off still another piece of flesh from his body. But the dove grew ever heavier. At the last, the King threw his whole body into the scale. And behold, the hawk and the dove disappeared, and in their place stood Indra and Agni, and they cried aloud: "Truly art thou a King, and knowest well the sovereign's first duty of protection! We have found thee more than we had heard. Thy body is no longer mangled. Live thou long within the hearts of thy people."[198]

It is true that these stories are told of kings, because they are regarded as the type of the Protector of the weak; but boys can also show protection, in a smaller measure, to all who are weaker than themselves. For these stories are told in order that we may take example by them and Copy in our own lives the virtues they describe.

The great type of *Compassion*—so that his compassion has passed into a proverb, "compassionate as Rantideva"—was again a King. Once he and his dependents went fasting for eight and forty days, and on the morning of the forty-ninth day he received some ghi, milk, barley, and water. To this frugal meal they sat down, when a Brahmana came as guest, and he fed him ere touching the food. Then when the Brahmana had departed, he divided what remained into equal shares, and gave to each, reserving one portion for himself. But as he prepared to eat, a Shudra came, and he gave him gladly a share of that small meal. And when the Shudra had gone, ere yet he could break his fast, a man came with a troop of dogs, and the rest of the food, save one drink of water, Rantideva gave to these. These also went, and Rantideva raised to his parched lips the welcome drink. "Give water, a little water," moaned a voice near by; and Rantideva, turning, saw a miserable form, an out- caste, lying on the ground, turning longing piteous eyes at the water in his hand. Bending over him, with sweet compassion beaming from his tender eyes, Rantideva gently raised the outcaste's head, and put the cool pure water to his panting dust soiled lips. "Drink, brother I" he said kindly doubling the value of the gift with his mild graciousness. And as the outcaste drank, the loving heart of Rantideva burst into prayer to Hari: "I do not

---

198 *Mahabharatam,* Vana Parra, cxxxic–xcvi; and Anushasana Parva, xxxii. The story is told of different heroic kings.

ask for the eight Siddhis," thus he spake.; "I do not ask Nirvana. Only I ask that I may pervade all beings, suffering for them their miseries, that they may live without sorrow. By giving this water to save the life of this suffering man, my hunger, thirst, languor, distress and giddiness have all passed away." And this prayer has ever remained the most perfect expression of compassion.

The danger which is connected with the shewing out of tenderness and protection to the weaker than ourselves is the vice of *Pride.* It arises from ahamkara, that gives the sense of separateness of "I" and "you," and thinks more of the fact that "I am helping this weaker one," than of sharing what is really a common store with one temporarily shut out from it by his separate form. By letting the mind dwell on one's own usefulness and power to do good, pride is awakened, and quickly ruins the good work that has been performed. None that wears a separate body may escape the power of this subtlest and most dangerous of foes, that is known as ahamkara. Even the very highest fall beneath its sway in unguarded moments and unavoidably suffer the consequences, for the Law of Karma is inflexible, and equal for high and low alike. Many a warning is therefore given in the Smriti against ahamkara and pride, the great and subtle foe of the wise and strong. Listen to some of these.

The ancient sage Narayana spent ages in the severest penance, on the peak known by the name of Badari of the Himalaya mountains. To test his freedom from the attractions of sense objects, Indra sent thousands of heavenly nymphs to play about in his Tapovana, his grove of austerity, and divert his attention away from his austerities. They did as directed. The Rishi Nrayana saw with his illumined eye the purpose of their coming and smiled with confidence. By his Yoga power he produced as many thousands of similarly shaped forms, and sent them forth to offer hospitality to Indra's hosts. The latter were ashamed, and prayed to the Rishi to forgive their evil purpose. He was pleased and did so, and further offered them a boon. And the boon they asked was that he should be their husband and protector. Great was his perplexity, but having said that he would give, he could not say no. He repented sadly; "This great trouble has arisen out of my ahamkara, without a doubt. The first cause of the frustration of all dharma is ahamkara." Then he said to the maidens: "It is against my vow to enter into the household life in this birth. In another birth, as Krishna, which I shall have to take for other work also, I shall redeem my promise, and bear the fearful weight of this huge household, marrying ye all out of the high families into which you also shall be born."

Vishvamitra, King of Gadhi, belonging to a line of Kshattriya Kings founded by Kusha, who came direct from BrahmA, returning to his kingdom with his armies after a great tour of conquest, passed through the Tapovana of the Sage Vashishtha. Leaving his armies at a distance, Vishvamitra went in reverence to the hermitage of the Sage to make obeisance. Vashishtha received him with all honour and kindness. As Vishvamitra rose to depart, fearing lest his armies cause disturbance in that place of peace, Vashishtha offered hospitality to the King with all his forces. Vishvamitra declined again and again, very unwilling to burden the ascetic's scant resources; but Vashishtha insisted again and again, intimating that by the powers of his tapas and with the help of his wonderful cow Nandini, he could with ease provide all that his regal guest could need for all his retinue. Thus in him arose ahamkara. Vishvamitra, thus over-pressed, consented, and beheld the wonders of the cow. Then greed arose in his mind, and he said: "What need has a Brahmana of such a cow: it is fit possession only for Kings," and he asked Vashishtha for the cow. Vashishtha then grew sad, but said:

Take the cow, if she consents to leave me." But the faithful cow would not; and when the men of Vishvamitra endeavoured to drag her away by force, then she appealed in piteous terms to her master not to abandon her. Then Vashishtha gave way to wrath, the natural next step after subtle ahamkara and pride, and a great war arose between the Brahmana and the Kshatrriya, which changed the whole history of the land. The cow called forth to her aid many non-aryan tribes, Shakas and Pahlavas, Yavanas and Barbaras, and they were destroyed by Vishvamitra; but finally the Brahmana power of Vashishtha overwhelmed the Kshattriya prowess of Vishvamitra: and, in vairagya, he gave up his kingdom and practised the severest tapas for ages, resolved to obtain the Brahmana power; and this he succeeded in doing, after long, long ages of self-denial, and peace was made between him and Vashishtha, and Vashishtha recognised him as a Brahmarshi.

To be King of the Devas is to hold a position that may easily fill the heart with pride, and from this cause Indra several times fell from his high estate. Once, surrounded by his Devas, he sat on the throne of the three worlds, and when Brihaspati, teacher of all the Devas, came before him, Indra kept his seat, not rising up to receive the great preceptor. Then Brihaspati turned and went his ways, abandoning the Devas, whom the Asuras then assaulted with success, driving them and their King from Svarga. This led to many another trouble, and to the slaying of a Brahmana on two several occasions by Indra, so that he had to perform much penance, ere he became purified.

Now, while Indra was performing this long penance, the Devas, in order that Svarga might not suffer the evils of anarchy, elected King Nahusha of the Lunar Dynasty of the earth's kings, to hold the high office of the Ruler of Heaven. None other was found fit for it. But, as Nahusha ruled, and ruled with greater might than Indra himself, pride grew in his heart from day to day, and thoughts of sin came into his mind behind the thoughts of pride. And he said to the Devas: "I bear the burdens of Indra, I must have his rights also. Let Shachi, the wife of Indra, appear before me." Then the Devas Spoke with each other in their distress, and thought that Nahusha was no longer fit to rule in heaven, and felt also Sure that the time for Indra's return was nigh. But who was strong enough to stand before Nahusha? The might that he had earned by past good deeds could be defeated only if he roused the wrath of some great Rishi by some dire offence. And so they spoke with Shachi, and told Nahusha that Shachi would see him if he came to her home on the shoulders of the Rishis. Nahusha ordered a conveyance borne by Rishis. And the sage Agastya and others were asked, by order of the King, to lift the sedan chair. And they consented gently. But, as the procession marched, Nahusha, in his eagerness and overflowing pride, touched Agastya's head with his foot arid angrily ordered him to go faster. Then Agastya saw that Nahusha's time was come, and he pronounced a curse on him, and Nahusha fell from heaven into a huge serpent's body on this earth, and suffered the pains of a high soul confined to a low body for many, many ages, till released therefrom by the wise words of his descendant, Yudhishthira, the King that had no enemy.

Now Bali, son of Virochana, had dwelt long in high prosperity, for the Devi Shri, or Lakshmi, abode with him as recompense for his good deeds. But pride in his own righteousness, and in the happiness it brought him, entered into his heart, and he began to think highly of himself and ill of others, and wrought evil to them instead of seeking their welfare as before. Then was the Devi displeased with Bali and determined to leave him, and to go and dwell with his enemy Indra, the Deva King in Svarga. And vainly Bali lamented his folly, when he saw the Devi, who had long blessed him, living with his rival. "And this," said Utatthya to King Mandhata, "is the result of malice and pride. Be thou awakened, O Man-dhata, so that the Devi of prosperity may not in wrath desert thee. The Shrutis declare that Unrighteousness begot a son named Pride on the Devi of Prosperity. This Pride, O King, led many among the Suras and the Asuras to ruin.

Many royal sages have also suffered destruction on his account. Do thou therefore awaken. O King. He who succeeds in conquering him, becomes a King. He who, on the other hand, suffers himself to be conquered by him becomes a slave."

Sometimes the inferior may save his superior, by his wise action, from falling into sin due to wrath and pride. Thus did a son save his father, in very ancient days. Chirakarin was the son of Gautama, of the race of Angirasa, and as his name implies—for Chirakara means acting slowly—he thought long ere he acted, and was very cautious and discreet. Now Gautama saw his wife commit a sin, and being very angry, he said to his son: "Slay this woman I" and went away. Then Chirakarin thought long how he should act, being compelled on the one side by the duty of obeying his father, and on the other side by the duty of reverencing the sacred person of the mother who bore him. "Obedience to a father's commands is the highest merit. Protection of the mother is a clear duty. How shall I, then, avoid sin? Son am I both of my father and mother. All that the son has the father gives. In his satisfaction, all the Devas are satisfied. His words of pleasure bring blessings to the son. But the mother? She is the giver of the body, the protector of the child. When the son loses his mother, the world for him is empty. Like her is no shelter, no refuge, no defence; none is so dear as she." Thus mused Chirakarin, bewildered by conflicting claims. Again he thought: "The husband has his names (Bhartri, Pati) as the supporter and protector of the wife. If he cease to support and protect, how shall he remain the husband? And my mother is to me the object of my highest reverence." Now Gautama, his mind calmed by meditation, was overwhelmed with the thought of the sin he had committed in commanding his son to slay his wife, and he hastened home, weeping, blaming his own carelessness for his wife's offence, and hoping that his son had not obeyed him. "Rescue me," he cried, thinking of his son, "rescue me and thy mother, and the penances I have achieved, as also thine own self, from grave sins." So it befell that Chirakarin, by his patience and careful consideration, did his father's real will though not his hasty order, and thus saved his father from a grievous sin, inspired by pride and wrath.

अहिंसायैव भूतानां कार्यं श्रेयोऽनुशासनम्।
वाक् चैव मधुरा श्लक्ष्णा प्रयोज्या धर्ममिच्छता॥

"Created being must be instructed for their welfare without giving them pain, and sweet and gentle speech must be used by a (superior) who desires (to fulfil) the sacred law."

रक्षणदार्यवृत्तानां कण्टकानां च शोधनात्।
नरेन्द्रास्त्रिदिवंयान्ति प्रजापालनतत्पराः॥

"By protecting those who five as Aryans, and by removing thorns, Kings, solely intent on guarding their subjects, reach heaven."

स्वे स्वे धर्मे निविष्ठानां सर्वेषामनुपूर्वशः।
वर्णनामाश्रमाणां च राजा सृष्टोऽभिरक्षिता॥

"The King has been created to be the protector of the castes and ashramas, who, all according to their rank, discharge their several duties."

यथोद्धरति निर्दाता कक्षं धान्यं च रक्षति।
तथा रक्षेन्नृपो राष्ट्रं हन्याच्च परिपंथिनः॥

"As the weeder plucks up the weeds and preserves the corn, so let the King protect his kingdom and destroy his foes."

सुवासिनीः कुमारीश्च रोगियों गर्भिणेस्तथा।
अतिथिभ्योऽग्र एवैतान् भोजयेदविचारयन्॥

"Let him, without making distinctions, feed newly-married women, young maidens, the sick, and pregnant women, even before his guests."

चक्रिणो दशमीस्थस्य रोगिणो भरिणः स्त्रियाः।
स्नातकस्य च राशश्च पंथा देयो वरस्य च॥

"Way should be made for a man in a carriage, for one who is above ninety years old, for a sick person, for one who carries a burden, for a woman, a Snataka, a King, and a bridegroom."

श्रनुक्रोशो हि साधूनामापद्धर्मस्यलक्षणाम्।
श्रनुक्रोशश्च साधूनां सदा प्रीतिं प्रयच्छति॥

"Compassion is the mark of the great merit of saints; compassion ever secures the blessings (or love) of the good."

न कामयेऽहं गतिभी श्वरात्परामष्टर्द्धियुत्त्कामपुनर्भवं वा।
श्रातिं प्रपद्येखिलदेहभाजामंतः स्थितोयेनभवन्त्य दु:खाः॥
क्षुतृट्श्रमो गात्र परिश्रमश्छ दैन्यं क्लमः शोकविषादमोहाः
सर्वेनिवृत्ताः कृपणास्यजंतोर्जिजीघिषोर्जावजर्लापणास्त्रे।

CHAPTER 11

THE RE-ACTION OF VIRTUES AND VICES ON EACH OTHER

We have now considered many virtues and vices separately, and have seen, in many illustrations, how virtues lead to happiness and vices to misery. We have finally to see how a virtue helps to produce a virtue in another, and a vice a vice, so that we may learn how to help others to rightness of thought and action, and thus promote their happiness. By showing love to others, we awaken love in them; by showing hate, we awaken hate. We are apt to feel as others feel. A man who is angry makes those around him angry, and so quarrels arise and grow more and more bitter. An angry word brings an angry reply, and that brings a still more. angry retort, and so on and on. On the other hand, gentle words bring gentle words in reply, kindness arouses kindness, and good deeds cause good deeds in others.

When this is understood, we can use right emotions to counteract wrong ones in others, instead of letting ourselves run into wrong emotions when these are shown to us. If a man speaks angrily to us, and we feel inclined to answer angrily, we should check ourselves and answer very gently, and this gentle answer will soothe him, and make him feel less angry. This is what is meant by returning good for evil, and only by acting in this way can we restore harmony when it is disturbed, and preserve it for the happiness of all.

When Draupadi urged King Yudhishthira to attack the Kurus, after he had been so cruelly cheated and ruined by them, the wise King pointed out to her that the returning of evil for evil could only result in the continuance of misery. "The wise man who, though persecuted, suffereth not his wrath to be aroused, joyeth in the other world, having passed his persecutor over with indifference. For this reason it has been said that a wise man, whether strong or weak, should ever forgive his persecutor, even when the latter is in straits...If amongst men there were not some equal to the earth in forgiveness, there would be no peace among men, but continued strife born of wrath. If the injured were to return their injuries, if one chastised by his superior were to chastise his superior in return, the consequence would be the destruction of every creature, and sin would prevail. If the man who hath ill speeches from another returneth those speeches; if the injured man returneth his injuries; if the chastised person chastises in return; then would fathers slay sons, and sons fathers; then would husbands slay wives, and wives husbands; then, O Krishna, how could birth take place in a world thus filled with anger? For know thou that the birth of creatures is due to peace."

Hear how Dasharatha, the King, turned away, by soft humility, the anger of his wife. Kaushalya, mother of Ramachandra, rent by anguish for the loss of that unequalled son, exiled for long years from her fond arms, spake for the first time angry words to Dasharatha: "Thou hast murdered thy sinless son with thine own hands, O King. Well hast thou trodden the Ancient Path, maintained by thy ancestors with so much toil. The husband is the first refuge of woman; the son is the second; the kinsmen the third; there is no fourth. Thou hast abandoned me; Rama is gone; I cannot leave thee here to go to him. In every way thou hast destroyed me, and destroyed the kingdom and the people." The King heard the harsh words, and bent lower under that greater burden of sorrow. His mind was all distraught, and he lost consciousness. Recovering, he saw Kaushalya still beside him. In that moment the memory of that past sin of his, of which this misery was the consequence, came back to him. Burning with the double sorrow of that sin and of the loss of Rama, trembling folding hands, and bending head, spoke to her: "Forgive me, O Kaushalya,. I fold my hands to thee. Ever wast thou tender-hearted, even untoothers, Bear with thy husband, whether he be good or ill. I am so broken already by my sorrow. Speak not harsh words to me, even in thy anguish." She heard that piteous speech of the humbled King, and tears of pity rushed forth from her eyes like new rain-water from the waterfalls. Her anger vanished, yielding place to deep humility and remorse and fear of sin for those harsh words. She seized the hands of the King, and. put them on her head, and in great agitation said: "Forgive, forgive me, O

King, I entreat thee with my head upon thy feet. It is for me to ask thee for forgiveness, not for thee to ask of me, for so great sin would come to me. That woman is not honoured of the wise in this or in the other worlds, who compels her husband to propitiate her, I know the dharma, and I know that thou, my husband, knowest it, and therefore must perforin thy promise and maintain the truth. Sorrow for my son drove me in a weak moment to say those words of wrong. Sorrow destroys all firmness; sorrow destroys all wisdom: there is no enemy like to sorrow. It swells within heart, like rivers in the rains, when I think of my beloved son." Thus was Kaushalya's bitterness overcome by Dasharatha's sweet humility and patience. If he had answered bitterly to her bitter words, the quarrel would have grown, and their common grief would have driven them from each other. But he met her pride with humility, her reproach with meekness, her anger with tenderness, and thus humility, meekness and tenderness were aroused in her.

So again does Ramachandra awaken trust towards Bharata in Lakshmana's angry breast, by showing out that trust Himself. Rama, gone forth from Ayodhya, with His wife and brother, to keep His father's word unbroken, dwelling in the forests, heard the distant murmurs of a marching army, and bade Lakshmana ascend a tree and look. Lakshmana saw that it was Bharata coming into the forest with a great throng of men. Anger at the exile forced his thought at once into the way of suspicion against Bharata, and he came in haste to Rama and asked him wrathfully to prepare for battle, as Bharata was coming to slay them and so make sure of his sovereignty. But Rama's mind was full of love to Bharata and not anger. And tenderly He said: "Mistrust him not. I will say to him: 'Give all this, kingdom unto Lakshmana,' and he will say but one word, 'Yes.'" The wrath of Lakshmana vanished, giving place to shame. And Bharata came and begged and prayed of Rama that he should go back to Ayodhya. But Rama would not break His father's word in letter or spirit. And Bharata carried away the walking sandals of Rama and placed them on the throne as symbol of the rightful Sovereign, and ruled Ayodhya in His name and as his regent, for the fourteen years of Rama's wanderings.

Over and over again in the dark days of their exile, did his wife and brothers, losing heart and patience, blame Yudhishthira for his loyal adherence to his compact with the Kauravas, and his patient endurance of wrong. Over arid over again did that noble heart, pierced and tortured by the reproaches of his loved ones, win them back by gentleness to the path of truth and honour. Thus Bhima, giving way to fierce anger, bitterly upbraid- ed his elder brother with "the trite merit of sticking to a promise" made to gamblers who had over-reached him, laid the loss of kingdom and riches at his door, reproached him with weakness, with deserting the virtues of his order, with making himself ridiculous. But Yudhishthira, summoning all his patience and remaining silent for a few moments, answered gently that doubtless all Bhima's words were true: "I cannot reproach thee for torturing me thus, piercing me with thy arrowy words; for from my own folly alone has this calamity fallen upon you all. I should have controlled my mind, and not have allowed it to be influenced by arrogance, vanity and pride. I cannot then reproach thee, O Bhima, for thy winged words. Yet have I given my pledge, and who may break his pledged word? Death is easier to bear than the gaining of a realm by a lie. What avail, then, to speak to me thus harshly? My heart is broken by the sight of the sufferings I have caused. But I may not break my word. Wait, O my brother, for the return of better days, as the sower waits for the harvest. For know, O Bhima, that my promise may not be made untrue. Virtue is better than life itself or than the joys of heaven. Kingdom, sons, fame, wealth, all these do not come up to one-sixteenth part of truth." Thus patiently did the prince bear his brother's angry taunts, and ever was he ready to meet harsh blame with gentle humility, and to win by love a yielding that his proud brothers would never have given to wrath.

As gentle, sympathy arouses love, so. does thoughtless ridicule arouse hatred, and hatred in its turn, gives rise to many evils. The fame of Yudhishthira spread far and wide, and all men praised the splendour of his Rajasuya sacrifice. Now this praise, bestowed on his hated rival, filled with jealousy the heart of Duryodhana, and. this evil emotion was rendered bitterer and more active by the careless disregard of his feelings shown by Bhima and by others; For one day as Yudhishthira was sitting on his golden throne, surrounded by his brothers, by many courtiers and Kings, Duryodhana and his brothers entered the assembly hall; and as he came he was deceived by the art of Maya, the Danava, who had built Yudhishthira's place with skill and craft, and taking the crystal lake as water, he drew up his garments to avoid wetting them, and later fell into water which looked like solid ground. Then Bhima laughed out boisterously and rudely, and others followed his bad example, although Yudhishthira reproved their lack of courtesy. And Duryddhana, with black frown, went away ashamed, with rage in his heart, and returned to Hastinapura, vowing vengeance for the insult; and this was one of the many causes that led at last to the gambling match and the exile, and the fierce battle of Kurukshetra, and the slaughter of Duryodhana and of his and Yudhisthira's kinsmen.

Evil returned with evil does but give birth to new evil, thus lengthening the chain of misery. Bhrigu had a son, Jamadagni, who became famous for his great austerities and rigid life, and in his family was born Rama, called later Rama of the Axe. Now Rama, though a Brahmana by birth, was at heart a Kshattriya, and his character was, as his grandfather Bhrigu had prophesied, "fit for the mil itary order;" and in Jamadagni also lurked hidden a seed of that fierce temper, which all his austerities had not availed to wholly burn away. And this caused sore trial and misery to befall this great race. For Jamadagni, furious at heart because of a hasty doubt of his wife's chastity, bade his sons, one by one, to slay her; but none would lift hand against the mother's sacred person save Rama, the youngest, who smote off her head with an axe. Being granted a boon by his father, he asked that his mother might be restored to life, and then went on pilgrimage to expiate the crime of matricide. But not thus could the evil wrought by Jamadagni's anger be exhausted. While her sons were absent, Renuka, the wife of Jamadagni, left alone, had to offer hospitality to Arjuna, son of Kritavirya; and he intoxicated with a warrior's pride, not deeming her reception worthy of his greatness, carried away forcibly the calf of the cow whose milk supplied the butter for the daily sacrifice. When Rama returned, Jamadagni told him what had happened, and the plaintive lowing of the cow for her young one increased the anger aroused by the recital; and so, losing self-control in passion, he rushed off and slew Arjuna, cutting off his thousand arms after fierce fight. This act aroused, in turn, fierce wrath of the kinsmen of Arjuna, and, to return evil with evil, they rushed to the hermitage of Jamadagni, where he sat engaged in meditation, and slew him with arrows, defenceless as he was, sitting immersed in contemplation. Nor yet was the tale of slaughter completed, since forgiveness—the only thing that could cut the chain of evil—was not in the heart of Rsma of the Axe; and he, having bewailed his father and having burned his body with due rites, vowed by that funeral pyre the slaughter of the Kshattriya caste—for thus the evil grew, ever swelling to larger and larger proportions. Then, taking up his axe, he attacked and slew the kinsmen of Arjuna, and after that warred with all Kshattriyas, exterminating well-nigh that warrior caste.

Even when we are treated with injustice and unkindness, it is best to preserve sweetness and agreeableness of behaviour, and thus win the one who so treats us, be he superior, equal or inferior, to show sweetness and agreeableness in return. Once Durvasa visited Duryodhana, and proved to be a very difficult guest to please. In vain did Duryodhana and his brothers, treat him with the greatest honour, waiting on him day and night. Sometimes Durvasa would say: "I am hungry, O King; give me some food quickly." And sometimes he would go out for a bath, and Duryodhana would have food prepared for his return, and on returning Durvasa would say: "I shall not eat anything to day, as I have no appetite." Coming suddenly, he would say: "Feed me quickly." And another time, rising at midnight, he would call for a meal, and when it was brought, would carp at it and refuse to touch it. Thus Durvasa, tormented Duryodhana for a while, but when he found that Duryodhana never showed either anger or impatience, then he became gracious to him and said: "I have power to grant thee a boon. Choose what thou wilt. Pleased as I am with thee, thou mayest obtain from me anything that is not opposed to religion or morals."[199]

Sometimes, indeed, a man is so hard-heart ed that no kindness can melt him, and then he goes on unyieldingly till, at last, he perishes. Duryodhana may serve as a striking illustration of this. Having robbed his cousins of their kingdom and riches and driven them into exile, Duryodhana resolved to feast his eyes on their poverty and hardships in the forest, advised by the wily Shakuni, who told him that, he would, increase his own joy by seeing the misery of his rivals; he took with him his brothers and friends and the royal ladies, that the Pandavas might suffer shame under the contrast. His cruel plot failed, in consequence of his being attacked and captured by the King of the Gandharvas.and his hosts, whom he had insulted in his overbearing pride. Some of the fugitives ran to King Yudhishthira and prayed his aid; the gentle King, rebuking Bhima for his (hitting words of refusal, bade his brothers arm themselves and rescue their kinsmen, remembering that, by the seizure of Duryodhana and the ladies of their house, the family honour was stained. "Entreated for help in such words as, 'Oh, hasten to my aid,' who is there that is not high-souled enough to assist even his foe, beholding him seeking shelter with joined hands. The bestowal of a boon, sovereignty and

199 *Mahabharatam*, Vana Parva, cxv—cxvil.

the birth of a son, are sources of great joy. But, O sons of Pandu, the liberation of a foe from distress is equal to all the three put together." So spake the high-souled King, and his brothers obeyed. The battle raged for some time, and then Arjuna and the King of the Gandharvas, who were friends, checked the struggle, and Arjuna enquired into the reason of the attack on Duryodhana. The celestial King explained that he knew Duryodhana's wicked motive in visiting the forest, and he was carrying him for punishment to Indra. Arjuna prayed his friend to set free the captives, at last the Gandharva King promised to do so, if Yudhishthira so wished, after hearing the whole story. The Pandava prince listened silently to the account of the mean and cruel outrage contemplated by Duryodhana, and thanking and praising the Gandharvas, he set Duryodhana and his companions free. When the Gandharvas were gone, Yudhishthira spoke lovingly to his cousin: "O child, never again do thou so rash an act, for rashness leads- never to happiness, O Bharata. O son of the Kuru race, blessed be thou with all thy brothers. Go back to thy capital as thou wilt, and be not thou sad or cheerless." Thus kindly did the blameless King treat his envenomed foe, the earthly author of his misery; but Duryodhana, departing, was only the more filled with grief and anger; the very kindness became a new offence, and he sullenly returned to Hastinapura, only hating the more bitterly those who had returned his evil with kindly aid.

Fortunately such doggedness in angry feeling is comparatively rare, for as the sun softens butter so does the warmth of kindly feeling soften the angry mood.

Even when anger shown to us arouses in us a corresponding feeling of anger, we may try to check it, and may refuse to give it expression in word, or look, or gesture. Such repression gradually extinguishes the feeling, and at least we have succeeded in not casting fuel on the flame to increase its burning. After some practice of this kind, we shall find that the anger of another no longer causes any feeling of anger in ourselves, and we shall be able to use all our strength in sending kind feeling to meet the harsh feeling of the other.

It is now easy for us to see why bad company should be avoided; if we are with people who are thinking unkind, or unclean, or other evil thoughts, or who are doing wrong actions—impure, intemperate, gluttonous acts—their feelings will work on us, and will push us towards thinking and acting in a similar way. Any evils of such kind as may lie hidden in ourselves will start into more active life under such influences, and will become stronger and more difficult to fight against. For these reasons a boy who wishes to lead a pure and industrious life at school, preparing himself for a noble and useful manhood, should avoid bad company, as much as he possibly can. And if at any time he is forced into it, so that he cannot escape, he should keep his mind very busy with pure and high thoughts, and thus try to affect those round him, and to influence them for good, instead of allowing himself to be influenced by them for evil. In this way we may turn our knowledge to good use, applying it to practice in our own lives, for thus only can we make our knowledge fruitful, and by noble living help to bring greater happiness to the world.

क्रुध्यन्तं न प्रतिक्रुध्येदाक्रुष्टः कुशलं वदेत्।

Let him not be angry again with the angry man; being harshly addressed, let him speak softly."

सेतूंस्तर दुस्तरान् श्राक्रोधेन क्रोधं सत्येतामृतंः॥

"Cross beyond the passes difficult to cross " beyond wrath by forgiveness; beyond untruth by truth.

श्रात्मानं च पराश्चैव त्रायते महतो भयात्।
क्रुध्यान्तमप्रति क्रुध्यन्द्वयोरेव चिकित्सकः॥

"He who is not angry with the angry, he is a physician unto both. He saveth himself as well as the others from great danger."

क्षमा ब्रह्म क्षमा सत्यं क्ष्मा भूतं साविं च।
क्षता तपः क्षमा शौचं क्षमयेदं धृत जगत्॥

"Forgiveness is truth, forgiveness is (source and support of) the past and the future. Forgiveness is tapas, forgiveness is purity; this world is upheld by forgiveness."

परश्चेदेनमतिबाणौर्भृशं बिध्येच्छम एवेह कार्यः।
संरोष्यमाणाः प्रत्तिहृष्यतैयः स श्रादते सुकृतं वे परस्य॥
श्राकृश्यमानो न वदामि किचित्।
क्षमाम्यहं ताडयमानश्च नित्यम्।
श्रेष्ठं ह्येतद्यतू क्षमामहुरार्याः
सत्यं तथैवार्जवमानृशस्यम्॥
श्राकुश्षमानो नकुश्येन् मन्युरेनं तितिक्षतः।
श्राक्रोष्ठारं निर्दहति सुकृतं चास्य विंदति॥
योनात्युक्तः प्राहरुक्षंप्रिय वायो वाहतो न प्रतिहन्तिधैर्यात्
पापचयोनेच्छतितस्यहन्तुस्तस्येहदेवाः स्पृहयन्तिनित्यम्
पापीयसः क्षमेतैव श्रेयसःयह्लशस्य च।
विमानितो हतोत्कुष्ठ एवं सिद्धिं गतिष्यति॥

"If a person deeply pierces a wise man with barbed words, the wise man should take refuse in patience. The man who, provoked to anger, only smileth back gently, not yielding to anger, he taketh away from the provoker all his merits.

"Spoken to harshly, I say nothing; even when assailed, I always forgive. This is the best—this that the elders have named forgiveness, and truth, and candour, and gentleness.

"Addressed harshly, let him not reply harshly. The wrath of the wrathful assailant consumeth himself, and taketh away all his merit.

"He that addressed roughly, answereth not roughly nor even mildly, he that being struck con- trolleth himself and returneth not the blow, nor wisheth ill unto the assailant, verily the pevas envy him.

"Abused, insulted, beaten, let him still forgive (all injuries) from the low and vile, from his superiors, from his equals; so shall he attain perfection " ''

आक्रुष्टस्ताडिता क्रुद्धः क्षमतेयो बलीयसः।
यश्च नित्यं जितक्रोधो विद्वानुत्तमपूरषः॥

"He indeed is the wise and good man who conquereth his wrath, and showeth forgiveness even when insulted, oppressed, and angered by a stronger."

यदि न स्युर्मानुषेषु क्षमिणाः पृथिवीसमाः।
न स्यात् संधिर्मनुष्याणां कोधमूलो हि विग्रहः॥
अभिषक्तो ह्यभिषजेदाहन्याद्गुरुणा हतः।
एवं विनाशो भूतानामघर्मः प्रेथितो भवेत्॥
आक्रुष्टः पुरुषः सर्वे प्रत्याक्रोशेदनन्तरम्।
प्रतिहन्याद्धतश्चैव तथा हिंस्याच्च हिंसितः॥
हन्युर्हि पितरः पुत्रान् पुत्रायचापि तथा पितृन्।
एवं संकुतिते लोके जन्म कृष्णो न विद्यते॥

[See p. 165.]

सर्वस्तरतु दुर्गाणिा सर्वो भद्राणिा पश्यतु।
सर्वः सुखमवाप्नोतु सर्वः सर्वत्र नन्दतु

ॐ सत्यं वद धर्मे चर
सत्यमेव जयते नानृतम् ॐ

"May all cross beyond the places hard to cross; may all behold good things; may all attain to happiness; may all rejoice everywhere."

"Aum ! Tell the Truth. Act the Right.

"Truth alone prevaileth, not Untruth. Aum !"

PEACE TO ALL BEINGS

Index

C

D

E

F

G

H

T

U

V

W

Y

LIST OF TITLES WITH ISBN NO.

ISBN	TITLE
9788194914129	1984
9789390575220	1984 & Animal Farm (2In1)
9789390575572	1984 & Animal Farm (2In1): The International Best-Selling Classics
9789390575848	35 Sonnets
9789390575329	A Clergyman's Daughter
9789390575923	A Study In Scarlet
9789390896097	A Tale Of Two Cities
9789390896837	Abide in Christ
9789390896202	Abraham Lincoln
9789390896912	Absolute Surrender
9789390896608	African American Classic Collection
9789390575305	Aldous Huxley: The Collected Works
9789390896141	An Autobiography of M. K. Gandhi
9789390575886	Animal Farm
9789390575619	Animal Farm & The Great Gatsby (2In1)
9789390575626	Animal Farm & We
9789390896158	Anna Karenina
9789390575534	Antic Hay
9789390896165	Antony & Cleopatra
9789390896172	As I Lay Dying
9789390896226	As You like it
9789390575671	At Your Command
9789390575350	Awakened Imagination
9789390575114	Be What You Wish
9789390896233	Believe In yourself
9789390896998	Best of Charles Darwin: The Origin of Species & Autobiography
9789390896684	Best Of Horror : Dracula And Frankenstein
9789390575503	Best Of Mark Twain (The Adventures of Tom Sawyer AND The Adventures of Huckleberry Finn)
9789390896769	Black History Collection
9789390575756	Brave New World, Animal Farm & 1984 (3in1)

9789390896240	Brother Karamzov
9789390575053	Bulleh Shah Poetry
9789390575725	Burmese Days
9789390896257	Bushido
9789390896066	Can't Hurt Me
9788194914112	Chanakya Neeti: With The Complete Sutras
9789390896042	Crime and Punishment
9789390575527	Crome Yellow
9789390575046	Down and Out in Paris and London
9789390896844	Dracula
9789390575442	Emersons Essays: The Complete First & Second Series (Self-Reliance & Other Essays)
9789390575749	Emma
9789390575817	Essential Tozer Collection - The Pursuit of God & The Purpose of Man
9789390896578	Fascism What It Is and How to Fight It
9789390575688	Feeling is the Secret
9789390575190	Five Lessons
9789390575954	Frankenstein
9789390575237	Franz Kafka: Collected Works
9789390575282	Franz Kafka: Short Stories
9789390575060	George Orwell Collected Works
9789390575077	George Orwell Essays
9789390575213	George Orwell Poems
9788194914150	Greatest Poetry Ever Written Vol 1
9788194914143	Greatest Poetry Ever Written Vol 1
9789390896301	Gulliver's Travel
9789390575961	Gunaho Ka Devta
9789390575893	H. P. Lovecraft Selected Stories Vol 1
9789390575978	H. P. Lovecraft Selected Stories Vol 2
9789390896059	Hamlet
9789390575022	His Last Bow: Some Reminiscences of Sherlock Holmes
9789390896134	History of Western Philosophy
9789390575121	Homage To Catalonia

9789390896219	How to develop self-confidence and Improve public Speaking
9789390896295	How to enjoy your life and your Job
9789390575633	How to own your own mind
9789390896318	How to read Human Nature
9789390896325	How to sell your way through the life
9789390896370	How to use the laws of mind
9789390896387	How to use the power of prayer
9789390896028	How to win friends & Influence People
9788194824176	How To Win Friends and Influence People
9789390896103	Humility The Beauty of Holiness
9789390896653	Imperialism the Highest Stage of Capitalism
9789390575084	In Our Time
9789390575169	In Our Time & Three Stories and Ten poems
9789390575145	James Allen: The Collected Works
9789390896189	Jesus Himself
9789390575480	Jo's Boys
9789390896394	Julius Caesar
9789390575404	Keep the Aspidistra Flying
9789390896400	Kidnapped
9789390896424	King Lear
9789390575824	Lady Susan
9789390896455	Law of Success
9789390896264	Lincoln The Unknown
9789390575565	Little Men
9789390575640	Little Women
9788194914174	Lost Horizon
9789390896462	Macbeth
9789390896929	Man Eaters of Kumaon
9789390896523	Man The Dwelling Place of God
9789390896349	Man The Dwelling Place of God
9789390575909	Mansfield Park
9788194914136	Manto Ki 25 Sarvshreshth Kahaniya
9789390896509	Marxism, Anarchism, Communism
9789390575664	Mathematical Principles of Natural Philosophy

9788194914198	Meditations
9789390575800	Mein Kampf
9789390575794	Memory How To Develop, Train, And Use It
9789390896486	Mind Power
9789390896585	Money
9789390575039	Mortal Coils
9789390575770	My Life and Work
9789390896035	Narrative of the Life of Frederick Douglass
9789390575152	Neville Goddard: The Collected Works
9789390575985	Northanger Abbey
9789390896530	Notes From Underground
9789390896547	Oliver Twist
9789390575459	On War
9789390575541	One, None and a Hundred Thousand
9789390896554	Othelo
9789390575435	Out Of This World
9789390575015	Persuasion
9789390575510	Prayer The Art Of Believing
9789390575091	Pride and Prejudice
9789390896561	Psychic Perception
9789390575381	Rabindranath Tagore - 5 Best Short Stories Vol 2
9789390575367	Rabindranath Tagore - Short Stories (Masters Collections Including The Childs Return)
9789390575374	Rabindranath Tagore 5 Best Short Stories Vol 1 (Including The Childs Return
9789390896622	Romeo & Juliet
9789390896127	Sanatana Dharma
9789390575596	Seedtime & Harvest
9789390896639	Selected Stories of Guy De Maupassant
9789390575206	Self-Reliance & Other Essays
9789390575176	Sense and Sensibility
9789390575299	Shyamchi Aai
9789390896738	Socialism Utopian and Scientific
9789390896646	Success Through a Positive Mental Attitude
9789390575428	The Adventures of Huckleberry Finn

9789390575183	The Adventures of Sherlock Holmes
9789390575343	The Adventures of Tom Sawyer
9789390896691	The Alchemy Of Happiness
9789390575862	The Art Of Public Speaking
9789390896288	The Autobiography Of Charles Darwin
9788194914181	The Best of Franz Kafka: The Metamorphosis & The Trial
9789390575008	The Call Of Cthulhu and Other Weird Tales
9789390575107	The Case-Book of Sherlock Holmes
9789390896110	The Castle Of Otranto
9789390896745	The Communist Manifesto
9789390575589	The Complete Fiction of H. P. Lovecraft
9789390575497	The Complete Works of Florence Scovel Shinn
9789390896820	The Conquest of Breard
9789390896813	The Diary of a Young Girl
9789390896332	The Diary of a Young Girl The Definitive Edition of the Worlds Most Famous Diary
9789390575701	The Great Gatsby, Animal Farm & 1984 (3In1)
9789390575312	The Greatest Works Of George Orwell (5 Books) Including 1984 & Non-Fiction
9789390575992	The Hound of Baskervilles
9789390896707	The Idiot
9789390896714	The Invisible Man
9789390575657	The Knowledge of the holy
9789390575558	The Law & the Promise
9789390896721	The Law Of Attraction
9789390896776	The Leader in you
9789390896363	The Life of Christ
9789390896196	The Man-Eating Leopard of Rudraprayag
9789390896783	The Master Key to Riches
9789390575268	The Memoirs Of Sherlock Holmes
9789390896479	The Midsummer Night's Dream
9789390575466	The Mill On The Floss
9789390896790	The Miracles of your mind
9789390896660	The Mutual Aid A Factor in Evolution
9789390896448	The Origin of Species

9789390896905	The Peter Kropotkin Anthology The Conquest of Bread & Mutual Aid A Factor of Evolution
9789390896806	The Picture of Dorian Gray
9789390896271	The Picture of Dorian Gray
9789390575275	The Power Of Awareness
9789390896356	The Power of Concentration
9788194824169	The Power of Positive Thinking
9789390575411	The Power of the Spoken Word
9788194914105	The Power Of Your Subconscious Mind
9789390896899	The Power of Your Subconscious Mind
9789390896417	The Principles of Communism
9789390575787	The Psychology Of Mans Possible Evolution
9789390896615	The Psychology of Salesmanship
9789390575732	The Pursuit of God
9789390575398	The Pursuit of Happiness
9789390896851	The Quick and Easy Way to effective Speaking
9789390575947	The Return Of Sherlock Holmes
9789390575138	The Road To Wigan Pier
9789390896981	The Root of the Righteous
9789390575855	The Science Of Being Well
9788194914167	The Science Of Getting Rich, The Science Of Being Great & The Science Of Being Well (3In1)
9789390896011	The Screwtape Letters
9789390896073	The Screwtape Letters
9789390575336	The Secret Door to Success
9789390575695	The Secret Of Imagining
9789390896868	The Secret Of Success
9789390896431	The Seven Last Words
9789390575930	The Sign of the Four
9789390896004	The Sonnets
9789390896516	The Souls of Black Folk
9789390896875	The Sound and The Fury
9789390575244	The State and Revolution
9789390896882	The Story of My Life
9789390896936	The Story Of Oriental Philosophy

9789390896752	The Strange Case of Dr. Jekyll and Mr. Hyde
9789390896943	The Tempest
9789390575916	The Valley Of Fear
9789390575879	The Wind in the willows
9789390896080	The Wind in the willows
9789390575763	Their eyes were watching gofd
9789390575831	Three Stories
9789390896950	Twelfth Night
9789390896592	Twelve Years a Slave
9789390896677	Up from Slavery
9789390896974	Value Price and Profit
9789390896967	Wake Up and Live
9789390896493	With Christ in the School of Prayer
9789390575602	Your Faith is Your Fortune
9789390575473	Your Infinite Power To Be Rich
9789390575251	Your Word is Your Wand
9789390575718	Youth
9789391316099	A Christmas Carol
9789391316105	A Doll's House
9789391316501	A Passage to India
9789391316709	A Portrait of the Artist as a Young Man
9789391316112	A Tale of Two Cities
9789391316747	A Tear and a Smile
9789391316167	Agnes Gray
9789391316174	Alice's Adventures in Wonderland
9789391316136	Anandamath
9789391316181	Anne Of Green Gables
9789391316754	Anthem
9789391316198	Around The World in 80 Days
9789391316013	As A Man Thinketh
9789391316242	Autobiography of a Yogi
9789391316266	Beyond Good and Evil
9789391316761	Bleak House
9789391316778	Chitra, a Play in One Act
9789391316310	David Copperfield

9789391316075	Demian
9789391316785	Dubliners
9789391316051	Favourite Tales from the Arabian Nights
9789391316235	Gitanjali
9789391316068	Gravity
9789391316150	Great Speeches of Abraham Lincoln
9789391316662	Guerilla Warfare
9789391316839	Kim
9789391316822	Mother
9789391316211	My Childhood
9789391316846	Nationalism
9789391316327	Oliver Twist
9789391316853	Pygmalion
9789391316334	Relativity: The Special and the General Theory
9789391316389	Scientific Healing Affirmation
9789391316341	Sons and Lovers
9789391316587	Tales from India
9789391316372	Tess of The D'Urbervilles
9789391316396	The Awakening and Selected Stories
9789391316402	The Bhagvad Gita
9789391316303	The Book of Enoch
9789391316228	The Canterville Ghost
9789391316907	The Dynamic Laws of Prosperity
9789391316006	The Great Gatsby
9789391316860	The Hungry Stones and Other Stories
9789391316433	The Idiot
9789391316440	The Importance of Being Earnest
9789391316297	The Light of Asia
9789391316914	The Madman His Parables and Poems
9789391316457	The Odyssey
9789391316921	The Picture of Dorian Gray
9789391316464	The Prince
9789391316938	The Prophet
9789391316945	The Republic
9789391316518	The Scarlet Letter

9789391316143	The Seven Laws of Teaching
9789391316525	The Story of My Experiments with Truth
9789391316532	The Tales of the Mother Goose
9789391316549	The Thirty Nine Steps
9789391316594	The Time Machine
9789391316600	The Turn of the Screw
9789391316983	The Upanishads
9789391316617	The Yellow Wallpaper
9789391316426	The Yoga Sutras of Patanjali
9789391316990	Ulysses
9789391316624	Utopia
9789391316679	Vanity Fair
9789391316020	What Is To Be Done
9789391316686	Within A Budding Grove
9789391316693	Women in Love